Robert Jones Burdette

**Chimes from a jester's bells**

Stories and sketches

Robert Jones Burdette

**Chimes from a jester's bells**
*Stories and sketches*

ISBN/EAN: 9783743367258

Manufactured in Europe, USA, Canada, Australia, Japa

Cover: Foto ©Andreas Hilbeck / pixelio.de

Manufactured and distributed by brebook publishing software (www.brebook.com)

Robert Jones Burdette

**Chimes from a jester's bells**

. . . Jump over the fence like a deer, run to beat Nancy Hanks for a half a mile and leap into the swimming-hole.  (Page 111.)

# CHIMES

FROM A

# JESTER'S BELLS

STORIES AND SKETCHES BY

## ROBERT J. BURDETTE

PART I. THE STORY OF ROLLO
PART II. STORIES AND SKETCHES

WITH ILLUSTRATIONS BY LOUIS BRAUNHOLD
COVER DESIGN BY ROBERT J. BURDETTE, JR.

INDIANAPOLIS AND KANSAS CITY

THE BOWEN-MERRILL COMPANY

M DCCC XCVII

TO MY

BEST FRIEND, GENTLEST CRITIC

TRUSTIEST COMRADE

ROBERT

THE SON OF HIS

MOTHER

# CONTENTS

# LIST OF ILLUSTRATIONS

# LIST OF ILLUSTRATIONS

# TO MY INKSTAND

Pierian Spring! Drowned in thy shallow deeps,
  Lie pearls of thoughts the world hath never known—
  Most of them other men's, but some mine own—
**The** worst **ones—over** which the sad Muse weeps
And thrusts back **to** thy darkest donjon keeps,
  Sinking them down with sable, bubbling moan,
  To drown in midnight horror, all alone,
Whiles a saved world unconscious round thee sleeps.
**In vain** I stain my **nose and ink my** thumb,
  And to the Ceiling-desert lift mine eyes,
Hoping from lime-wash, sub-lime thoughts to drink;
My shallow murmurs make the deep more dumb;
  Jet black beneath my vexing pen it lies—
**I have it now!** Great snakes! There goes the ink!

# CHIMES FROM A JESTER'S BELLS
## THE STORY OF ROLLO

# ALPHA

IGHT.

Silence.

A struggle for the light. And he did not know what light was. An effort to cry. And he did not know that he had a voice.

He opened his eyes, "and there was light." He had never used his eyes before, but he could see with them.

He parted his lips and hailed this world with a cry for help. A tiny craft in sight of new shores; he wanted his latitude and longitude. He could not tell from what port he had cleared; he did not know where he was; he had no reckoning, no chart, no pilot.

He did not know the language of the inhabitants of the planet upon which Providence had cast him. So he saluted them in the one

universal speech of God's creatures—a cry.
Everybody—every one of God's children, understands that.

Nobody knew whence he came. Some
one said, "He came from heaven." They
did not even know the name of the little life
that came throbbing out of the darkness into
the light. They had only said, "If it should
be a boy," and, "If it should be a girl."
They did not know.

And the baby himself knew as little about
it as did the learned people gathered to welcome him. He heard them speak. He had
never used his ears until now, but he could
hear with them. "A good lusty cry," some
one said. He did not understand the words,
but he kept on crying.

Possibly he had never entertained any
conception of the world into whose citizen-
ship he was now received, but evidently he
did not like it. The noises of it were harsh
to his sensitive nerves. There was a man's
voice—the doctor's, strong and reassuring.
There was a woman's voice, soothing and
comforting—the voice of the nurse. And one

was a mother's voice. There is none other like **it**. It was the first music he heard in this world. And the sweetest.

By and by, somebody laughed softly and said in coaxing tones,

"There—there—there—give **him** his dinner."

His face was laid close against the fount **of** life, **warm** and white **and** tender. Nobody told him **what** to **do**. Nobody taught him. He knew. **Placed** suddenly **on** the guest-list of this changing old caravansary, he knew his way at once to two places in it— his bed-room and the dining-room.

Wherever **he came from** he must have made a long journey, for **he was** tired and hungry when he reached here. **Wanted** something to eat right away. **When** he got **it**, he went to sleep. Slept **a** great deal. When he awoke, he clamored again, in the universal volapük, for refreshment. Had it, and went to sleep again.

**When he** grew older, the wise men told him **the worst** thing **in** all this world, of many good and **bad** things that **he** could do, was

3

to eat just **before** going to sleep. **But the** baby, not having learned the language of the wise men, **did** this very worst of all bad things, and, having no fear of the **wise** men, defiantly **throve** upon it.

**He** looked young, but made himself **at home** with the easy assurance **of an old trav**eler. Knew the best room in the house, demanded **it, and** got **it.** Nestled into **his** mother's arms **as** though **he** had been measured **for** them.

Found that "gracious hollow that God · **made"** in his mother's shoulder that fit his **head as** pillows **of** down never could. Cried when they took him away from it, when he was **a** tiny baby "with no language but **a** cry." Cried once again, twenty-five **or** thirty years afterward, when God took **it** away from him. All the languages he had **learned,** and all the eloquent phrasing **the** colleges had taught him, **could not then voice the sor**row of his **heart so well as the** tears he tried **to** check.

Poor little baby! Had to go to school the first **day** he got here. Had to begin his

4

lessons at once. Got praised when he learned them. **Got** punished when he missed **them.**

Bit his own toes and cried when he learned there was pain **in** this world. Studied the subject forty years before he learned in how many ways suffering **can be** self-inflicted.

Reached for the moon and cried because he couldn't get it. Reached **for** the candle and cried because he could. First lessons in mensuration. Took **him fifty or** sixty years of hard reading to learn **why** God put so many beautiful things out of our longing reach.

Made everybody laugh long before he could laugh **himself,** by going into **a** temper because his clothes didn't fit **him or** his dinner wasn't served promptly. "Just **like a man,"** the nurse said. Nobody in the family could tell where he got his temper. Either **he** brought it with him, or found it wrapped and addressed to his room when he got here. **At** any rate, he began to use it very shortly after **his arrival.**

Always said he lost his temper, when most

certainly he had **it** and was using **it**.   Played
so  hard  sometimes  that  **it**  made  him  **cry.**
Took him  **a**  great many  years  to  learn that
too much play is apt to make anybody cry.

**By** and  by,  he  learned  to  laugh.   That
came  later  than  some  **of the**  other  things;
much  later  than  crying.   It  is  a  higher **ac-**
complishment.   **It**  is  much  harder  to  learn,
and  much harder to do.   He never cried unless  he  wished, and  felt **just** like **it**.   But he
learned  to  laugh,  many,  many times  **when he**
wanted  to  **cry.**

**Grew so, after** awhile, that **he**  could laugh
with  **a**  heart  **so** full **of**  tears they  glistened in
his  eyes.   Then  people  praised his  laughter
the  most—"**it** was  in  his  very  eyes,"  they
said.

Laughed, one baby day, to see **the** motes
dance in the sunshine.   Laughed at them once
again,  though  not  quite  **so**  cheerily,  **many**
years later, when he discovered they were only
motes.

**Cried,** one baby day, when he was tired of
play and  wanted **to** be  lifted  in  the  mother
arms and sung to sleep.   Cried again one day

6

when his hair was white, because he was tired of work and wanted to be lifted in the arms of God and hushed to rest.

Wished one-half his life that he was a man. Then turned around and wished all the rest of it that he was a boy.

Seeing, hearing, playing, working, resting, believing, suffering and loving, all his life long he kept on learning the same things he began to study when he was a baby.

# ROLLO LEARNING TO BREATHE

## I

HEN Rollo was a very little boy, so small, indeed, that his feet did not reach one-third of the way down to the hem of his long white dress, which reached only half way to the floor, Rollo's father, who never considered it a hardship—to himself—to tap his reservoir of learning at any time, and let a stream of wisdom flow forth to irrigate the sterile intellectuality of adjacent mankind, said to Rollo's mother:

"My dear, I think it is about time that Rollo should be taught to speak English and breathe through his nose."

Rollo's mother, at that moment, was conversing with Rollo's father's son in a strange,

uncombed language with a limited vocabulary and a vast number of terminations in
"ie," insomuch that her remarks sounded
very much like the catalogue of what was
formerly known in the United States as a
"Female Seminary."

For a moment, as is the manner of a
woman entertaining a baby, Rollo's mother
continued steadfastly to ignore Rollo's father,
the sun, moon, and stars, the seas and all
that in them is, the earth and the heavens
above it, as complacently and tranquilly and
happily as though there were but two creatures in all the universe—a mother and a
baby.

The effect of this treatment varies upon
different subjects. A woman understands it,
and does not mind it; in fact, even though
she never had a baby of her own, she enters
into the rhapsody with all her heart. But
men are otherwise affected. A narrow-minded
man it makes jealous; a conceited man it
irritates; it makes an ambitious man thoughtful; a right-minded man it amuses. He

rather enjoys it, especially if he has a **pater-nal** interest **in the** infant monopoly.

**At** length, without withdrawing **her** eyes from **the baby, Rollo's** mother found time to **reply to** Rollo's father, in a mere parenthesis. **She** said, or seemed to say, as though her thoughts were far, far away from her **words :**

" I never heard **of** a baby breathing through its nose."

Being only **a** woman, **she** had **never heard of a** great many things pertaining **to** babies, which **are** matters of commonplace informa-**tion among** men. **Then, speaking** to the **baby and at** her husband **with** great **animation and** intense earnestness, she added :

"Whassie is he ittie mousie-wousie made for if **he** hassie beezie soo **he** nosie-wosie? Wansie beezie soo his ittie mousie-wousie, so he doesie—bessums!"

**At** this **Mr.** Holliday, **who was Rollo's** father, turned pale **and caught hold of his** hair with both hands, and held **himself firmly in** his chair. Thus **he** doubtless prevented himself **from** committing assault with intent to **do** bodily **harm. Mr.** Holliday was **a**

kind-hearted man, although a philanthropist. But he was also a very wise man, and he knew that the social position which he occupied—which is now termed, by those Americans who make money by note and spell by ear, the "upper middle class"—did not permit him to correct the women of his household with that freedom enjoyed by the more highly privileged aristocracy and the lower classes. (Pronounced clawsses.)

The environment of the unhappy "upper middle class" is indeed very narrow. Freedom lies beyond either of its boundaries, above or below. Either Shaun McGonegal or the Duke of Astorbilt may sit down to his dinner in his shirt sleeves; either the Prince or Knuck Buncoman may give shady banquets with police court supplements, and the standing of these actors, in their respective social scales, is not affected. But a bookkeeper with a large family and a small salary, or a preacher, must wear a white shirt and a most uncomfortable collar, even in the sacred privacy of home life. The luxuries of moral and social undress are either too cheap or too expensive for the " upper middle class."

**Mr.** Holliday knew this; indeed he knew about everything that one man could know on the same day, and he explained it to Rollo's mother, although much he doubted if she understood him. However, he was not a man to be disturbed by a little thing like that. The sound of his own voice, even in his stormiest moments, had a soothing effect upon him. Sometimes, when alone, he would set his mouth going, and sit in his chair with his eyes closed, listening to it, as one listens to sweet and inspiring music.

"The healthy child," said Mr. Holliday, "instinctively breathes through its nose until it is misled by false teaching and incorrect training by incompetent women."

"The first thing any child does," replied Rollo's mother, "is to open his mouth wide as he can, and cry for half an hour louder than a full-grown man can shout. He has no use whatever for a nose except to snuffle with."

"Well," said Mr. Holliday, "that is because it is a baby and has no more sense. But he is now old enough to know better, and I am not going to have him grow up with the lower part of its face open all the time like a fish out of water. He shall breathe properly, or I shall not allow it to breathe in my presence. And you must not encourage him in his shiftless disposition to breathe with the greater part of its facial anatomy and two-thirds of the organs of speech and rudimentary mastication."

So saying, Mr. Holliday said to Rollo firmly, but kindly:

"Now, Rollo, close your mouth and inhale the atmosphere by filtration through the nasal passages; do you hear?"

Rollo blinked his eyes to express that he heard, and, opening his mouth somewhat wider than it was before, breathed through it as easily as though he had had a steady job of breathing for ten years instead of ten months.

His father was a man not to be trifled with. He was a new man, who wore bloomers and knew that the old-fashioned ideas about children were all wrong, and that **a** child's education should begin as soon as his intelligence is sufficiently developed to enable him to discern when **he is** hungry, or when the nurse from the agricultural, mechanical and chemical training school for advanced nurses of the higher nursing has fastened his garments to the flesh of his **back** with a safety-pin. **He** said:

"Rollo, you must not trifle with **me. You** understand what **I** say **very well; if you do** not, **you must ask me to** repeat my remarks **more** distinctly and **in simpler** language, which **is** not at all necessary. I will not humor you **in** any childishness. Now, once more, I command you to close your lips and perform the operation of breathing through the nasal orifices."

So saying, he placed his hands **on Rollo's** mouth. **A** muffled **roar** followed, **and Rollo's** face **became purple.** Rollo's father **took** his hand away **to see** what caused the discoloration. Rollo immediately followed **up** the advantage gained by his childish ruse. By a sudden act of inhalation he filled

14

. . . . "*I command you to close your lips and perform the operation of breathing through the nasal orifices.*" *So saying he placed his hands on Rollo's mouth.* (Page 14.)

his lungs with about ninety-six cubic inches of complemental air, then, deftly depressing **the** rear of the cricoid cartilage—he stretched the vocal cords to their utmost tension, which he knew would produce the high, shrill note most effective for his purpose. He then released the strain upon his **costal** cartilages, sent a volume of air up the trachea and through the organs of phonation, whence it issued from his wide-open mouth **in a yell** which even Mr. Holliday, **who** knew **more than he** could carry at one time, afterward admitted he had never heard equaled.

Instantly reversing the action of the expi-**ratory** muscles and bringing **into** violent action **the** muscles **of** inspiration, Rollo quickly re-filled his lungs (the **two** saccular organs occupying the thorax**),** and repeated the former operation.

This, when continued for any length of time, is called ''fretting,'' by grandmothers; ''weeping,'' by aunts; ''crying,'' by mothers; ''howling,'' by fathers; ''yelling,'' by uncles; ''squalling,'' by big brothers, and **a** great many things which very few can spell

15

and nobody should pronounce, by the neighbors.

In a short time Rollo's father was out of
sight, having seized his hat and hastened
away to consult an eminent aurist, whose
name the ethics of his profession forbids to
us to print. This is forbidden, indeed, by
the ethics of two professions—journalism and
medicine. The ethics of journalism demand
from 40 to 250 cents a line, in advance.
These ethics are hard to get over.

After teaching Rollo to breathe, Mr. Holliday said he had a note to pay that would
keep him busy in his laboratory, inventing
excuses, for the next four years, and he would
permit Rollo's mother to teach his son to
speak the English language correctly.

Rollo's mother, left to her own methods,
taught her little son to mangle the English
grammar even seven times more than it
was wont to be mangled by the wise men
who invented it. She taught him to speak
correctly in twenty-five or thirty easy lessons
every day.

Rollo's mother was a painfully ignorant

woman. She had no knowledge of training a child by the carpenter-shop, boiler-room, and general machine-shop methods.

She thought the baby's instructions in house ventilation, practical plumbing, village sanitation, mining engineering, the care of the sick, general sewage, water filtration, mind cure and applied hypnotism might be deferred with safety until his seventh year, at least.

Poor woman! She had a foolish, old-fashioned notion, six or seven thousand years old, that a baby was a sweet little bundle of helplessness, something to coddle and cuddle, and coo over. So she talked to her baby in "ie's" and "sh's" until she nearly drove Mr. Holliday mad, and Rollo picked up the language with wonderful precocity, such is the natural depravity of the human race. Mother and baby could read each other's faces, and Rollo would crow, or coo, laugh or look serious, in faithful reflection of the face that bent over him. It was a poor, weak, antiquated method, far, far behind the hot-house and forcing-room system. But it suited Rollo, and he learned all the time.

What dreams he had when he pillowed his dimpled face upon her snowy breast; what confidences they had in the silly talk of baby land when he woke and held long conversations of "ah-goo, ah-google, ah-googelie, google ah-goo," he never told.

But it drew them very close to each other. Pain was soothed, trouble was driven away, and fears allayed, the sun shone and the birds sang when the mother eyes looked down at him and the mother lips rained soft kisses and baby nonsense upon his face.

So Rollo lay in his mother's lap, content, happy, studious; learning more and more every day, giving new inflections and startling variations to his original tongue by sucking his thumbs in the midst of the "goo ah-gooing," while with his chubby feet—his mother called them "tootsie wootsies," from the stronghold of her lap, he kicked brave defiance at all the baby-building in this scientific, half-taught old world of fads.

A world that never did, and never does,

and never will offer a baby anything **one-half so** good, **and** sweet, and helpful, **and instructive, as** old-fashioned **mother-love, without a freak,** frenzy, or ism **in it.**

## SPELL AND DEFINE:

| | | |
|---|---|---|
| Paregoric | Googlglgl | Insomnia |
| Omniscience | Incomprehensibility | **Pedestrianism** |
| Man | Spoon-food | Nocturne |

What is **meant by** "cerebral activity?"—In **how many** men **does** this develop **before death?—Name** one.—How many scales has a fish?—An opera?— Why did Rollo's father consult an aurist?—What is an **aurist?—Has** an **ass** more ears than a man?—Why **not?—How** many men think they know as much as **Rollo's father**?—Name the exception.—And what was **the cause of his** death?—**What is** meant by "rats"?

# ROLLO LEARNING TO DRESS

## II

NE morning, while Rollo was still sufficiently, or rather more than sufficiently, inconsiderate of his father's feelings and wishes to remain somewhat of a baby—although a great many wise people, who never had any babies, insisted that he was quite old enough to begin to take care of himself and assist his father a little about the house—his father said:

"Rollo, I think you are taking up too much of your mother's time in the morning, compelling her, not only to assist you in making your toilet, but even to place upon your person, and fasten in its place, every article of your apparel. **I am** sure you are sensible enough to realize that you are too old to be so young as you would have been had you not been born until a later period of your existence—say sometime during the month subsequent, or even in the following year. **You were born on** the tenth of April; and **I** know a great many boys who **were not** born **until late in** September—some, even **in** the closing week **of** December—who are **at** this time nearly sixteen years old, pursuing their studies at school or learning useful trades at which they will ultimately be able to strike several times **a** year; and here you are, yet lingering **in** your **second** year.

" **I** am willing to allow **you** reasonable time to grow **up, but** you must not waste too much of your life **in** idle and unproductive infancy. You have now been a child for a year and a half. Doctor Bonedust, **A. B.,** A. M., Ph. D., LL. D., who called on me yesterday to ascertain when **I was** going **to** send you to school, told me that, when he **was** your age, **he wore** pantaloons and could strap **a razor**, although I believe he **did** not begin to shave himself until some years **after-wards**."

"I don't believe," said Rollo's mother, " **that** Doctor Bonedust ever was so young as **Rollo**. **He** may have been as small, early **in** his life, but I think he was as old when **he** was born as he is to-day."

But Mr. Holliday said, somewhat sternly, that such a remark was unworthy of any sane person; all human beings, he said, at some time during their lives **were** infants **for a** longer **or** shorter period.

**Still Rollo's mother** insisted that **she** knew some **people** who **may** have **been** infants, as, **in** their maturer years they continued to be, **but** they never had been babies, which was something altogether different. No one, she **averred, who** had ever been a baby **even for a little** while, entirely outgrew **the con-**dition of babyhood. She read **in a** history **of** the war—the large **one**, which she used **to block** the **front** door **open—how** soldiers, great bearded men, strong and brave, struck **down** by the terrible bullets on the battle-field, cried "Mother!" as they fell to their

22

death. And other soldiers, dying of wounds
**in** the white-walled hospitals, passed away
moaning " Mother, mother! " as though they
were children again, and there was but one
hand and one voice in all the world could
soothe the cruel pain that was killing them
hour by hour.

All men, she said, **were** babies **all their**
lives, if they had ever been babies at **all,** and
had had real mothers; and especially **if** they
had had an aunt and a grandmother. Any
woman who ever had the care **of** a **grown**
man on her hands knew this. Rollo's mother
blushed **a** little as she concluded her speech,
which was an unusually long one **for** her, and
Rollo's father **looked** at **her for a moment** in
mute astonishment. **Then** he said:

"**It is** not becoming **in** me to pursue a subject so frivolously treated. **To** resume my
remarks by returning **to** them, I think Rollo
should now learn to dress himself. And as I
know your partiality will not permit you to
**be** sufficiently firm with him, you may go
down stairs and leave him with me."

" **You** may have to help him a little with

23

some of the hard things," she said, turning as she passed out the door, with a look that fell across the cradle like a bar of sunshine. Rollo answered the look with a joyous shout in their own language, to which his mother nodded a reply, and then left him alone with that good and wise man, his father.

"Now, Rollo," said Mr. Holliday, "it is time for you to arise and put on your garments. Get up and dress yourself, my son," he added, kindly translating his remark into what he considered absolutely puerile baby talk, "Come!"

A brief interval of silence followed, during which Mr. Holliday investigated a number of singular-looking garments of Lilliputian dimensions, which were arranged for his son's toilet. He gave an ejaculation of astonishment as he lifted the child from his cradle and placed him in the big bed which Rollo had learned to regard as his campus and gymnasium. Then he turned and shouted toward the open door, in the voice of an elocutionist shouting to a deaf man in the adjacent settlement—

24

"Look here! Talk about dressing this child! Why, he has on more clothes now than I wear to town! What under the sun do you do with all the things he sleeps in?"

The rustle of a woman's dress, which rose quite near the door and faded away down the hall, would have indicated to the female mind that Rollo's father was expending an undue amount of vocal force in addressing Rollo's mother, and that she was, indeed, making an offing at that moment before she answered the hail.

Even the baby's face, as it turned in the direction of the half-audible sound with surprising quickness, showed that Rollo was aware that his mother had not gone into neutral waters, but was standing by and large within reach of his signals. Her message came drifting back.

"Take off everything he has on!"

As the music came floating into the room, Rollo gave a little crow, and looked at the door as though he might see the musician follow.

"Your mother is not going to dress you

this morning, Rollo," said his father, interpreting the expectant look with masculine penetration. "I am going to teach you to dress yourself, and will render you only such assistance as may be absolutely necessary."

He shook out the smallest article of infantile garmenture he could find, and, after examining it minutely, cried—

"Which goes on first?"

There was no answer from any direction, and he turned to his son and said:

"Rollo, I will not endure to be trifled with much longer. Do you know, or rather, will you tell me, which is the top end of this thing? H'm? What? Why do you not answer me? What is this which I hold in my hand?" he went on, in the tone of a prestidigitator performing the second-sight act with a silver watch borrowed from the subject for the occasion—"speak quickly, Rollo. I wish to know if your mother calls these two rudimentary sleeves, which appear to be united by a strip of some woven fabric, a shirt? H'm? You will not tell me? Very well, then; you may put it on without know-

"*I am going to teach you to dress yourself, Rollo. . . Show papa which side goes on before, and then papa will show you which side goes behind.*" (Page 27.)

ing what it is. **Put it on, Rollo; that's** papa's good boy. **Show** papa which side you put on before, and then papa will show you which side goes behind!''

Rollo looked **up** into **his father's face, and,** twisting one thumb into his mouth to assist his articulation, ''google-ah-gooed'' with great fluency, removing his thumb **now and** then to say '' papa '' and '' ma'ma,'' **and to** make **a** few soft noises imitative of the dialect **of** the domestic pets and barnyard cattle **and** fowls, displaying decided excellence and originality in reproducing the song of the cow, and the gentle challenge of **a** soft-voiced, peace-loving rooster **on a** Quaker **farm at** Kennett Square.

Rollo's father listened for **a** moment, looking as wise as a woman listening to the **Latin** oration at a college commencement. **(A man** does not look wise under this cataract of erudition. He looks foolish, as though he had been caught listening to something he had no business to hear.**)**

Presently **Mr.** Holliday said:

'' **Very** well; **if you** will not begin without

some assistance, Rollo, I will help you a little, but you must not expect me to do everything for **you,** as **your** mother does. Now—keep still, **Rollo; you** must be patient or you will **never** learn to dress yourself—you must not fidget **in** that manner, Rollo; you must be— keep still! How ever am I going to get your head and **arms** through a thing that has no hole in **it** when you **try to** put them **all** through at once? Any woman who would— keep your head still, Rollo!—make a straight jacket **like** this for a—ROLLO!—Christian **child to** wear ought **to** be—hold still!—sent **to** the insane—WHAT are you trying to do?

" Sit still!

" Put out your foot!

" The other one—the other one—THE OTHER ONE! Doesn't the child know which **is** his other foot?

" **Turn** around! **The other way! This way!**

" Sit down!

" Stand up!

" **Oh,** Saint Sebastian! that pin went clear through my thumb!

28

"Hold up your head! HOL DUP **PURE RED**! Do you understand that?

"Hold your leg straight! This one!

"What lunatic tied this string full of knots? **How in** the **name of** common sense is a man expected to fasten **a** thing that has no buttons?

"Put out your hand! **Turn** around!— Shut up your noise! Stand still! **Oh,** murder! There's another pin!

"Don't wave your arms about that way! This isn't a swimming school.

"ROLLO!

"**Put** out your **foot**!

"Hold **your** leg stiff!

"Here!" **he** roared, turning toward the door, "Come **up** stairs, quick! What'd **I** tell you! **You've** ruined this **boy** for life! He hasn't a **sound** bone or normal joint in his body! Every one of them works both ways! You've made a helpless cripple **of** him forever by your foolish woman's coddling!"

Before his appeal for help was ended, Rollo's mother **was** in the room, with such suddenness **as** fairly startled Mr. Holliday, whose

**29**

nerves were somewhat strained by recent experiences.

**She saw** Rollo sitting **in** the middle **of** the **bed** with his arms tightly manacled to the **sides of** his head by **a** twisted shirtlet which crossed **his** face in many folds, concealing **from** sight **all his** features save **two** tear-brimmed blue eyes, and at the same time **even** of the most primitive character.

"**Well,**" said Mr. Holliday, defensively, "that's the way he **told** me **it** went **on!**"

**She gave** a little reassuring laugh with an inflection **of** amusement in **it, bent** over the baby, gave the rebellious garment a gentle twist, a shadow **of a** touch, a feint at a jerk, and there it was on the plump little body as though it grew there.

She drew a pair of shapeless stockings over two legs that had **just enough knees in** them **to keep** the dimples from spilling **out.** She gave **a** pat here **and a** caress there; she smoothed this **and** folded that, **and** all the while she cooed and the baby crowed. Presently Mr. Holliday said:

"I now perceive, Rollo, that you can go on by yourself with the assistance I have given you. I hope you will be dressed in time for breakfast, and I trust it will never again be necessary for me to assist you in making your morning toilet."

And, indeed, Mr. Holliday's wisdom was justified of herself; he was never cast for that part again.

Half an hour later, when that good man went to the breakfast table, he was pleased to see the little boy sitting in his high chair, completely dressed, his face washed till it shone like the day, his hair neatly brushed, his eyes bright as the morning-glories peeping in at the window. Mr. Holliday bent to kiss the restless little head as he went to his own seat. And through the blessing that morning, Rollo played a lively accompaniment on his plate with his spoon, while in a bird-like voice he sang a sweet little hymn, the words and music of which he had composed himself:

"Goo-gool googabbl obbl ma'ma goodl oodloo oo,
Gobbl-owa bawawa gooba papa obbly goobl awa!"

31

And really it made the bread as sweet as
Mr. Holliday's more formal grace.

## SPELL AND DEFINE:

| Pin | Button | Knot |
| --- | --- | --- |
| Labyrinthine | Noncomatibus | Womanly |
| Perforation | Exclamatory | Snarled |

Can a man fasten anything with a pin?—Why not?—
How does a woman pin a glass knob on a bureau
drawer?—In a shad weighing four pounds, there are
957,639,257,000 bones; how many, then, are there in a
man weighing 157 pounds?—What is the age of a
baby?—Analyze and parse the following sentence—"If
he had of known what difficulties he would of encoun-
tered, he would not of attempted it."—Of what part of
speech is "of"?—Of what part of man are his clothes?
If so, how many?—Name three.

# ROLLO LEARNING TO READ

## III

HEN Rollo was five years young, his father said to him one evening:

"Rollo, put away your roller skates and bicycle, carry that rowing machine out into the hall, and come to me. It is time for you to learn to read."

Then Rollo's father opened the book which he had sent home on a truck and talked to the little boy about it. It was Bancroft's History of the United States, half complete in twenty-three volumes. Rollo's father explained to Rollo and Mary his system of education, with special reference to Rollo's learning to read. His plan was that Mary should teach Rollo fifteen hours a day for ten years, and by that time Rollo would be half through the beginning of the first volume, and would like it very much indeed.

Rollo was delighted at the prospect. He cried aloud:

"Oh, papa! thank you very much. When I read this book clear through, all the way to the end of the last volume, may I have another little book to read?"

"No," replied his father, "that may not be; because you will never get to the last volume of this one. For as fast as you read one volume, the author of this history, or his heirs, executors, administrators, or assigns, will write another as an appendix. So even though you should live to be a very old man, like the boy preacher, this history will always be twenty-three volumes ahead of you. Now, Mary and Rollo, this will be a hard task (pronounced tawsk) for both of you, and Mary must remember that Rollo is a very little boy, and must be very patient and gentle."

The next morning after the one preceding it, Mary began the first lesson. In the be-

34

ginning she was so gentle **and** patient that her mother went away and cried, because she feared her dear little daughter was becoming **too** good for this sinful world, and might soon spread her wings **and** fly **away and be an** angel.

But in the space **of a** short time, the novelty **of** the expedition wore off, and Mary resumed running her temper—which **was of** the old-fashioned, low-pressure kind, just forward of the fire-box—on **its** old schedule. When she pointed to " A " for the seventh time, **and** Rollo said " W," she tore the page **out by** the roots, hit her little brother such a **whack over** the head with the big book that **it set** his birthday **back six** weeks, slapped him twice, **and** was just going **to** bite him, when her mother **came in.** Mary told her that Rollo had fallen **down** stairs **and** torn his **book** and raised that dreadful lump on his head. This time Mary's mother restrained her emotion, and Mary cried. But it was not because she feared her mother was pining away. **Oh, no; it** was her mother's rugged health **and virile** strength that grieved Mary,

35

as long as the seance lasted, which was during the entire performance.

That evening Rollo's father taught Rollo his lesson and made Mary sit by and observe his methods, because, he said, that would be normal instruction for her. He said:

"Mary, you must learn to control your temper and curb your impatience if you want to wear low-neck dresses, and teach school. You must be sweet and patient, or you will never succeed as a teacher. Now, Rollo, what is this letter?"

"I dunno," said Rollo, resolutely.

"That is A," said his father, sweetly.

"Huh," replied Rollo, "I knowed that."

"Then why did you not say so?" replied his father, so sweetly that Jonas, the hired boy, sitting in the corner, licked his chops

Rollo's father went on with the lesson:

"What is this, Rollo?"

"I dunno," said Rollo, hesitatingly.

"Sure?" asked his father, "You do not know what it is?"

"Nuck," said Rollo.

"It is A," said his father.

36

" Huh," said Rollo, "I knowed that letter." "Then why did you not say so," replied his father so sweetly that Jonas, the hired boy, sitting in the corner, licked his chops. (Page 63.)

" A what? " asked Rollo.

" A nothing," replied his **father**, "it is just A. Now, **what is it?** "

" Just A," said **Rollo.**

" Do not be flip, my son," said **Mr. Holli-**day, " but attend to your lesson. **What let-**ter is this? "

" I dunno," **said Rollo.**

" Don't fib **to me**," said his father, gently, " you said a minute **ago that** you knew. That is **N.**"

" Yes, sir," replied Rollo, meekly. Rollo, although **he** was a little boy, was no slouch, **if he** did wear bibs; he knew where he lived without looking **at the** door-plate. When it came time **to be** meek, there was no boy this side of the planet Mars **who** could **be meeker,** on shorter notice. **So he** said, " Yes, sir," with that subdued **and well** pleased alacrity of **a** boy who has just been **asked** to guess the answer to the conundrum, " **Will** you have another piece of pie? "

" Well," said his father, rather suddenly, " what **is it?** "

" **M,**" said **Rollo,** confidently.

"N!" yelled his father, in three-line Gothic.

"N," echoed Rollo, in lower case non-pareil.

"B-a-n," said his father, "what does that spell?"

"Cat?" suggested Rollo, a trifle uncertainly.

"Cat?" snapped his father, with a sarcastic inflection, "b-a-n, cat! Where were you raised? Ban! B-a-n—Ban! Say it! Say it, or I'll get at you with a skate-strap!"

"B-a-m, band," said Rollo, who was beginning to wish that he had a rain-check and could come back and see the remaining innings some other day.

"Ba-a-a-an!" shouted his father, "B-a-n, Ban, Ban, Ban! Now say Ban!"

"Ban," said Rollo, with a little gasp.

"That's right," his father said, in an encouraging tone; "you will learn to read one of these years if you give your mind to it. All he needs, you see, Mary, is a teacher who doesn't lose patience with him the first

38

time he makes a mistake. Now, Rollo, how do you spell, B-a-n—Ban?"

Rollo started out timidly on c-a—then changed to d-o,—and finally compromised on h-e-n.

Mr. Holliday made a pass at him with Volume I, but Rollo saw it coming and got out of the way.

"B-a-n!" his father shouted, "B-a-n, Ban! Ban! Ban! Ban! Ban! Now go on, if you think you know how to spell that! What comes next? Oh, you're enough to tire the patience of Job! I've a good mind to make you learn by the Pollard system, and begin where you leave off! Go ahead, why don't you? Whatta you waiting for? Read on! What comes next? Why, croft, of course; anybody ought to know that—c-r-o-f-t, croft, Bancroft! What does that apostrophe mean? I mean, what does that punctuation mark between t and s stand for? You don't know? Take that, then! (whack). What comes after Bancroft? Spell it! Spell it, I tell you, and don't be all night about it!

39

Can't, eh? Well, read it then; if you can't
spell it, read it. H-i-s-t-o-r-y-ry, history;
Bancroft's History of the United States!
Now what does that spell? I mean, spell
that! Spell it! Oh, go away! Go to bed!
Stupid, stupid child," he added as the little
boy went weeping out of the room, "he'll
never learn anything so long as he lives. I
declare he has tired me all out, and I used to
teach school in Trivoli township, too. Taught
one whole winter in district number three
when Nick Worthington was county superintendent, and had my salary—look here,
Mary, what do you find in that English
grammar to giggle about? You go to bed,
too, and listen to me—if Rollo can't read that
whole book clear through without making a
mistake to-morrow night, you'll wish you
had been born without a back, that's all."

The following morning, when Rollo's father
drove away to business, he paused a moment
as Rollo stood at the gate for a final good-
bye kiss—for Rollo's daily good-byes began

at the door and lasted **as long as his father**
was in sight—Mr. **Holliday said :**

"**Some day,** Rollo, you will thank **me for**
teaching you to read."

"Yes, sir," replied Rollo, respectfully, **and**
then added, "but not this **day.**"

Rollo's head, though **it had here and there**
transient bumps consequent **upon foot-ball**
practice, **was not** naturally **or permanently**
hilly. On the contrary, **it** was **quite level.**

SPELL **AND** DEFINE:

| | | |
|---|---|---|
| **Tact** | Imperturbability | Ebullition |
| Exasperation | Red-hot | Knout |
| Lamb | Philosopher | Terrier |

Which end of **a rattan hurts the** more?—Why does
reading make **a full man?—Is** an occasional whipping
good for a boy?—At precisely what age does corporal
punishment cease to **be** effective?—And why?—State,
in exact terms, how much better are grown up people
without the rod, than little people with it?—And why?—
When would a series of good sound whippings have
been of the greatest benefit to Solomon, when he was
**a** godly young man, or an idolatrous old one?—In or-
**der to** reform this world thoroughly, then, whom
**should we** thrash, the children **or** the grown-up people?—**And why?**—If, then, the whipping post should

41

LEARNING TO READ

be abolished in Delaware, why should it be retained in the nursery and the school room?—Write on the board, in large letters, the following sentence:

If a boy ten years old should
be whipped for breaking a window,
what should be done to a man
thirty-five years old for breaking
the third commandment?

42

# ROLLO LEARNING TO WORK

## IV

NE day when Rollo was about nine years old, his father said to Rollo's mother that it was about time that boy was beginning to earn his salt.

When Rollo heard this, he was very much pleased, and so expressed himself. Because, if there was anything in the list of edible foods which he liked less than all the rest, it was salt. Therefore, he reasoned with himself, if his salt was all he was expected to earn, he could amass enough of that to last him all his life, merely by working between times, when he was tired of thinking what he would like to play at next.

Without giving all his reasons, therefore,

Rollo said to his father that he was very glad indeed it was time for him to earn his salt, as he thought, perhaps, he might use less of it if he had to earn it.

His father looked at him earnestly for a moment, as though he was undecided whether to reply to his little son, or say something. He decided upon the alternative and bade Rollo accompany him.

Rollo followed his father down the path that ran by the side of the house. He found a large, resonant torpedo in his pocket, left over from the Fourth of July. Being an economical boy—thanks to the careful teaching of his wise and prescient father—Rollo did not wish to waste the torpedo. Therefore he threw it at his Uncle George's fox terrier, which lay curled up asleep on the doorstep.

The terrier was having bad dreams, evidently, for just as the torpedo reached him and exploded, he sprang to his feet with a loud and commingled chorus of startled yelps and angry barks, in the manner of a dog that finds himself surrounded by hostile foes with belligerent intentions.

The noise attracted the attention of Rollo's Uncle George, who was sitting in his room up stairs reading. Rollo's Uncle George was a *Haverford* man, and consequently read all the time he was not doing anything else. Rollo's great ambition was to grow up and be a man just like his Uncle George. And Rollo's father, who loved his brother-in-law dearly, said that he probably would, if he never grew any older than he was now.

This pleased Rollo very much indeed. When he repeated his father's encouraging remark to his Uncle George, Uncle George laughed also, the hollow, mocking laugh of a man in pain.

Hearing the fox-terrier, Uncle George leaned far out of the window so suddenly that he knocked off his high silk hat, which, being a senior, he wore all the time. The hat fell in the path directly in front of Rollo's father, who, not seeing it—this being his near-sighted day—kicked it over the flowering current bush, and it fell into the wheelbarrow where Thanny, Rollo's little brother, was playing. Thanny immediately threw himself flat on the hat, and shouted in childish glee, "down!" Thanny was a very little boy, who was too young to know that a hat was not a foot ball. He then punted it to Rollo, who passed it up to the window, shouting as he did so, "our ball, Uncle George!"

Rollo did not understand what Uncle George said, but supposed it had reference to some of the new plays known only to students.

In the meantime, his father had brought a large, glistening cylindrical object from the kitchen porch.

"Now, Rollo," said Mr. Holliday, for it was indeed he, "here is a nice little watering pot which your mother and I bought you for a birthday present."

It was indeed a very fine watering pot, made of galvanized iron, capable of holding

46.

about eight gallons, and had painted upon it in large red letters:

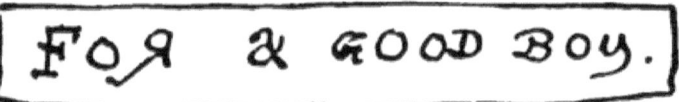

The letters had been hand-painted by Jonas. Jonas made very nice large, plain letters, and his custom of printing the letter R backward made his work very difficult to counterfeit.

"So you see, Rollo," said Mr. Holliday, "if ever you should lose your little sprinkler you can easily identify it, if you should recognize it, when you recover it." "Water," continued Mr. Holliday, speaking, "weighs ten pounds to the gallon, when drawn from a country well, and perhaps twice as much when taken from a city hydrant. That will make your little watering pot, when filled, weigh about ninety-four pounds, which is not very much for a great boy like you to lift. I would carry it myself were it not that my old wound, which I received in both legs while carrying despatches from the battle

field to Washington, during the battle of Bull
Run, is troubling me again to-day."

A gurgling kind of a chuckling noise from
the window of Rollo's Uncle George's room
indicated that Uncle George was reading a
funny book, and had, or had not, quite forgotten his anger about the accidental mistakes which incidentally had happened to
happen to his hat. Uncle George, being a hard
student, read a great many funny books "to
take the strain off his mind," he said. Rollo's father said the constant strain on Uncle
George's mind was probably what pulled it
out so thin.

"And here, Rollo," said his father, "is
the pump."

"Is this the pump?" exclaimed Rollo, in
tones of great surprise.

"Yes," replied his father, with the pleased
and complacent air of a man who is reveal-
ing a great secret, "this is the pump. Now,
in order to procure water for drinking, culi-
nary or toilet purposes, you must raise the
liquid from the bottom of the well by suction,
which you will produce by agitating the

48

handle of the pump in a perpendicular **manner,** alternately raising and lowering **it.''**

"What is alternately?" asked Rollo, **who was a** very intelligent boy and was fond of asking many, very many—oh, **a** very great many—questions preparatory **to** beginning any piece **of** work in which **he** felt **no** restless desire to engage. He wished to know all **about** the work, **he** said, before he began, and **then he** could go at **it** advisedly. **He did not** care, he said, **if it** took all **day to learn** about it. He never considered it fatiguing—not very fatiguing, that is—to hear his father talk, **when** Rollo was **at** liberty to select the **topic of** conversation.

Conversation, in the Holliday family, was a term applied **to a favorite** family diversion, or occupation, **of** looking wise **while Mr.** Holliday improved the time.

"Alternately," replied Rollo's father, "means 'in reciprocal succession.'"

Rollo's Uncle George's merry laugh rang out **in a** clear, many-syllabled volley from **the open** window.

Rollo wished **he** knew what he was laugh-

ing at. He determined to ask him at dinner.

"Reciprocal suck session," repeated Rollo, in order to fix the definition firmly in his
mind, so that he would know what he was
doing when he was pumping. "That is how
I get the suck shun on the water."

"Naw," snarled Mr. Holliday, pleasantly,
"it isn't! Don't you know anything? It
means by turns; you first push the pump-
handle down—down, as far as it will go; then
you lift it up as high as you can. See?"

"But it is down, now," said Rollo.

"Well, then," replied his father, "you
first lift it up."

"But," persisted Rollo, "you said just
now that I must push it down; and now
again you say I must first lift it up. Must I
push it down and raise it up both at once,
the first time?"

Mr. Holliday gasped, but controlled himself as they heard Rollo's Uncle George come
to another joke in his book, and said, very
patiently:

"Little stupid! No! If the handle is

already **down,** you first lift **it up,** but **if it** is up, then you must first push **it** down, and afterward keep up that regular alternation of motion **or** action.''

'' Keep it up and down, don't you mean?'' asked Rollo.

'' Yes-s-s-s!'' said **Mr.** Holliday, **between** his teeth, as though **his** old **wound were** clinching him with renewed agony. '' Keep moving **the** handle **up** and **down** in alternation !''

''In reciprocal suck session? '' said Rollo.

'' Yes, my son,'' said Mr. Holliday, so **sweetly** that Rollo backed off two or three steps. '' Yes-s! I am glad to see that you have **such an** intelligent comprehension of the method **of** procuring water **by** the common suction pump.''

'' Is the other kind **of pump** easier **to** work? '' asked Rollo.

'' No,'' replied his father, '' **it is a** great deal harder. Now—''

'' But,'' exclaimed Rollo, with the eagerness **of** an industrious boy, **as he** saw his father placing the **water-pot under the nose**

51

of the common suction pump, "what if I should find **the** pump-handle half-way up and half-way **down?** '

"**In** that case," replied his father, "**it would not** make any difference **which** way **you** started. **Now,** here is the—"

"But if I should start it wrong," exclaimed Rollo, who was prudent far beyond his years, and was really very anxious to **learn to work,** but **wanted** to learn **correctly,** "that is, **if I** should **push the** handle **down when I** ought to lift **it up,** and raise **it up** when **I** should **push it down, would** that make **it pump** the wrong **way, and pump all** the water I had already pumped **up, back** into **the well** again?"

"No!" yelled Mr. Holliday, quietly, "of course not. Any lunatic would know better than that. After you **get** fairly **started it** doesn't **matter** how **you work** it"

"Then," said Rollo anxiously, **as** though **all these** possible contingencies disturbed him **in his** impatience **to** get **to** work, "**if I** stopped pumping and went into the house to **get a** drink, it wouldn't do any harm if, when

I came back, I should forget which **way I** had left the handle sticking?"

"Why, **you** little numbskull," shouted **Mr.** Holliday, with painstaking distinctness, "couldn't **you** see **which way it was** when **you** came back?"

"Yes," said Rollo, "but that might not **be the way I** left **it; it** might have slipped **down, or** jumped up, and I wouldn't want **to** begin **on** the wrong stroke and maybe **blow** up the pump."

Mr. Holliday turned black in the face and reached his right hand out toward the peach tree, but just at that moment Uncle George came **to a "corker"**—that **was** what he called **it—in his book, and** burst **into** such **a** shriek of **laughter as made them** both **look** toward the window.

"That's a dandy book Uncle George is reading," said Rollo wistfully, "I'll bet it isn't the 'Memoir of John Mooney Mead.'"

"It is some worthless trash," replied Rollo's **father,** and then continued, **as** he stood **back to let Rollo** get **to** the **pump,** "now, **my** son, let **me** see you—"

"Does it make any difference," asked Rollo, "which hand I pump with first?"

"No," howled his father, thoughtfully, "but if you don't take hold of it with one hand or the other quicker'n scat I'll take hold of you with both hands in a way that you'll remember after you've forgotten how old you are. PUMP!"

He shrieked the word with such explosive suddenness that the fox terrier sprang to his feet with a frightened bark and looked suspiciously at Rollo, while Uncle George, who seemed to have finished his book and taken up his music lesson, could be heard singing something that ended with a college yell.

"Is that Italian?" asked Rollo, who had a fine ear for music.

"Yes; it's English opera Eyetalian," roared Mr. Holliday, who never lost patience with children, for he knew they must be taught very lovingly. "Yes! Now get hold of that pump and shake her up for first water, or I'll shake the bones out of you. Pump!"

Rollo seized the pump-handle with both

54

hands, and, raising it as high as he could, **stood** holding it arm's length above **his** head.

" This **way?**" he asked.

"Yes, that way!" snorted his father, very sweetly, indeed, for he was pleased to see how rapidly Rollo was learning to work.

" Yes, that way. Well," **he** shouted, as Rollo stood holding **the** handle **high in** the **air, " are** you going **to** stand there **all** day? **Get a** wiggle **on you!** Bring **it** down, **I** tell you!"

" **But** it won't come down," replied Rollo, " **I am** pushing as hard as ever I can."

" Pull **it** down then! Pull it, you little moosie!" yelled **Mr.** Holliday **in** soft, patient tones. " Haven't **you got** the little sense you **were born** with? **If you go** out alone you'll get drawn **on** the jury. Pull **it down!**"

" But," said Rollo, still holding the handle above his head, " you said I must first raise it up as high as it would go, and then push it down; you didn't say anything about pulling it down. I can't hold it up here much longer, either," **he** said. And, indeed, he was growing **very red in** the **face. So** was his father.

" Well, **you** hear me tell you now," roared **Mr.** Holliday, smiling until Rollo could **see the** manufacturer's trade-mark on the roof of **his** natural teeth. " Pull it down! Here! This way! Git away from the pump!"

As Mr. Holliday, for it was he who addressed him, made a rush at him, Rollo, who was quite active **for a** boy of only nine years, **let go the pump-handle and** dodged.

**It was an** old-fashioned, Early English pump-handle, **made of iron,** about five feet long, quite gracefully curved, with a round Queen **Anne** knob **on** the end, somewhat larger than a base-ball, though of course not quite so hard. As Mr. Holliday came within range, and Rollo "let go **all** holts," **as he** afterward explained to his sister Mary, **being in** fear of bodily injury—because **he** had seen his father " monkeying," **as** Rollo called it, with the peach tree—the Elizabethan handle **came** down on the run, the Queen Anne knob catching **Mr.** Holliday on the top of the head with a most awful and resounding thwack—

56

*They clustered in a mournful little group at the foot of the pump, Mr. Holliday leaning limply against it.   (Page 57.)*

Rollo said it was a "sockdollager," but his Uncle George, whose vocabulary was perfectly Shakespearean, said it was a "sollaker"—which, to quote from Uncle George's report, " grassed him."

They clustered in a mournful little group at the foot of the pump, Mr. Holliday sitting down and leaning limply against it, while Rollo, and his sister Mary, and Uncle George asked Rollo's father questions, which they immediately answered themselves. Soon they were joined by Rollo's mother, who, hearing them in conversation, came out " to see what they were having such a good time about."

When they told her she tried to look pleasant.

" I am so sorry," she said, her sweet voice vibrant with sympathy, " that you did not tell me this was going to happen. Were you trying to get water out of that pump?"

As Mr. Holliday could only nod his head diagonally, which might mean either yes, or no, or both, or neither, and Uncle George was too busy rubbing on the witch hazel to answer, Rollo said:

"Yes, at least—that is—I was."

"Well," replied Rollo's mother, "you must not do so any more, because the man took the rod out of it yesterday to mend the sucker. He said it did not work very well."

But Rollo said that it seemed to work quite easily to-day. And then, as his father made a movement to rise, Rollo went away; not very far away—just about four miles down Mill creek, over the hill the other side of Humphrey's mill, up past Fairview school, and so out to Montgomery pike and around by Ardmore, home again.

SPELL AND DEFINE:

| | | |
|---|---|---|
| Arnica | Sucker | Student |
| Toil | Bunco | Erudition |
| Investigation | Soldier | Yell |

At what speed does light travel ?—What is the highest velocity ever reached by a man working by the day ?—Has this record ever been broken ?—Two boys start from the same point at the same time, one going to school, the other to the "Old Swimmin' Hole"; which arrives first at his destination ?—Yes. And

why ?—How many miles **farther** does he have to go ?
—Yes. And why does **he run** while the other boy
walks ?—Which of these two boys will grow up to be
a good and great man ?—And why ?—What becomes
of the other boy ?—And why ?—Would you rather remain at home and dig plantain and dandelions out of
the lawn than go a-fishing with **the other** boys ?—And
why ?—What is the doom of all liars ?

## V

ARLY in the afternoon of the same day, Mr. Holliday came home bearing a large package in his arms. Not only seldom, but rarely, did anything come into the Holliday homestead that did not afford the head of the family a text for sermonic instruction, if not, indeed, rational discourse. Depositing the package upon a hall table, he called to his son in a mandatory manner:

"Rollo, come to me."

Rollo approached, but started with reluctant steps. He became reminiscently aware as he hastily reviewed the events of the day, that in carrying out one or two measures for the good of the house, he had laid himself open to an investigation by a strictly partisan **committee,** and the possibility of such an inquiry, with its subsequent report, grieved **him.** However, he hoped for the worst, so that in any event **he** would **not be** disagreeably disappointed, and came running to his father, calling " Yes, sir!" **in his** cheeriest tones.

This **is the correct** form in **which to** meet any possible **adversity which is not yet in** sight. Because, **if it** should not meet **you, you are** happy anyhow, and if it should meet you, you have been happy before the collision. **See?**

"**Now, Rollo,**" said **his father,** " you are too large **and** strong **to be** spending your leisure time playing **baby games** with your little brother Thanny. **It** is time for **you to** begin to be athletic."

" What is athletic? " asked **Rollo.**

"Well," replied his father, who was **an** alumnus (pronounced ahloomnoose) himself, "**in a** general way **it** means **to** wear a pair of **pantaloons** either eighteen inches too short or six inches too long for you, and stand around and yell while other men do your playing for you. The reputation for being an athlete may also be acquired by wearing a golf suit to church, or carrying a tennis racket to your meals. However, as I was about to say, I do not wish you to work all the time, like a woman, or even a small part of the time, like a hired man. I wish you to adopt for your recreation games of sport and pastime."

Rollo interrupted his father to say that indeed he preferred games of that description to games of toil and labor, but as he concluded, little Thanny, who was sitting on the porch step with his book, suddenly read aloud, in a staccato measure.

"I-be-lieve-you-my-boy,-re-plied-the-man-heart-i-ly."

"Read to yourself, Thanny," said his father kindly, " and do not speak your syllables in that jerky manner."

Thanny subsided into silence, after making two or three strange gurgling noises in his throat, which Rollo, after several efforts, succeeded in imitating quite well. Being older than Thanny, Rollo, of course, could not invent so many new noises every day as his little brother. But he could take Thanny's noises, they being unprotected by copyright, and not only reproduce them, but even improve upon them.

This shows the advantage of the higher education. "A little learning is a dangerous thing." It is well for every boy to learn that dynamite is an explosive of great power, after which it is still better for him to learn of how great power. Then he will not hit a cartridge with a hammer in order to find out, and when he dines in good society he can still lift his pie gracefully in his hand, and will not be compelled to harpoon it with an iron hook at the end of his fore-arm.

Rollo's father looked at the two boys attentively as they swallowed their noises, and then said:

"Now, Rollo, there is no sense in learning to play a man's game with a toy outfit. Here are the implements of a game which is called base-ball, and which I am going to teach you to play."

63

So saying he opened the package and handed Rollo a bat, a wagon tongue terror that would knock the leather off a planet, and Rollo's eyes danced as he balanced it and pronounced it a "la-la."

"It is a bat," his father said sternly, "a base-ball bat."

" Is that a base-ball bat? " exclaimed Rollo, innocently.

"Yes, my son," replied his father, "and here is a protector for the hand."

Rollo took the large leather pillow and said :

" That's an infielder."

"It is a mitt," his father said, " and here is the ball."

As Rollo took the ball in his hands he danced with glee.

"That's a peach," he cried.

"It is a base-ball," his father said, " that is what you play base-ball with."

"Is it?" exclaimed Rollo, inquiringly.

"Now," said Mr. Holliday, as they went into the back yard, followed by Thanny, " I will go to bat first, and I will let you pitch, so that I may teach you how. I will stand here at the end of the barn, then when you miss my bat with the ball, as you may sometimes do, for you do not yet know how to pitch accurately, the barn will prevent the ball from going too far."

"That's the back-stop," said Rollo.

"Do not try to be funny, my son," replied his father, "in this great republic only a President of the United States is permitted to coin phrases which nobody can understand. Now, observe me; when you are at bat you stand in this manner."

And Mr. Holliday assumed the attitude of a timid man who has just stepped on the tail of a strange and irascible dog, and is holding his legs so that the animal, if he can pull his tail out, can escape without biting either of them. He then held the bat up before his face as though he was carrying a banner.

"Now, Rollo, you must pitch the ball directly toward the end of my bat. Do not pitch too hard at first, or you will tire yourself out before we begin."

Rollo held the ball in his hands and gazed

**at it** thoughtfully **for a** moment; he turned **and looked at the** kitchen windows as though **he had half a mind to** break one **of** them; **then** wheeling suddenly he **sent** the ball **whizzing through** the air like **a** bullet. **It** passed **so** close **to Mr.** Holliday's face that he dropped the bat and his grammar in his nervousness and shouted:

"Whata you throw nat? That's no **way** to pitch a ball! Pitch **it** as though you were playing **a** gentleman's **game; not as** though **you were trying to** kill **a cat!** Now, pitch it **right here;** right at this **place on my** bat. And pitch more gently; the first thing **you** know you'll sprain your wrist and have to go to bed. Now, try again."

This **time** Rollo kneaded the ball gently**,** as though he suspected **it** had been pulled **be-** fore it was ripe. He made an offer **as** though **he** would throw **it to** Thanny. Thanny made **a** rush **back to an** imaginary "first," and Rollo, turning quickly, fired the ball in the general direction of Mr. Holliday. It passed about ten feet to his right, but none the less **he made what** Thanny called " a swipe " at it that turned him around **three** times before he could steady himself. It then hit the end of the barn with **a** resounding crash **that** made Cotton Mather, the horse, snort with **terror** in his lonely stall. Thanny called **out in a** nasal, sing-song tone:

"Strike—one!"

"Thanny," said **his father, severely,** "do **not let me** hear a repetition of such language **from** you. **If** you wish **to** join **our game,** you **may** do so, if you will play in a gentle-manly manner. But **I** will not permit the use **of** slang about this house. Now, Rollo, that was better; much better. But you must aim more accurately and pitch less violently. You will never learn anything until you acquire **it,** unless you pay attention while giving your mind to **it.** Now, play ball, as **we** say."

This time Rollo stooped and rubbed the ball in the dirt until his father sharply repri-manded him, saying, "You untidy boy; that ball will not be fit to play with!" Then Rollo looked about him over the surrounding country as though admiring the pleasant view, **and with the** same startling abruptness as be-

fore, faced his father and shot the ball in so
swiftly that Thanny said he could see it smoke,
It passed about six feet to the left of the bats-
man, but Mr. Holliday, judging that it was
coming "dead for him," dodged, and the
ball struck his high silk hat with a boom like
a drum, carrying it on to the "back-stop"
in its wild career.

. "Take your base!" shouted Thanny, but
suddenly checked himself, remembering the
new rules on the subject of his umpiring.

"Rollo!" exclaimed his father, "why do
you not follow my instructions more carefully?
That was a little better, but still the ball was
badly aimed. You must not stare around all
over creation when you are playing ball.
How can you throw straight when you look
at everything in the world except the bat
you are trying to hit? You must aim right
at the bat—try to hit it—that's what the
pitcher does. And Thanny, let me say to
you, and for the last time, that I will not permit the slang of the slums to be used about
this house. Now, Rollo, try again, and be
more careful and more deliberate."

" Father," said Rollo, " **did you** ever play **base-ball when** you were a young man?"

" **Did I** play base-ball?" repeated his **father,** " did I play ball? Well, say, I belonged **to the** Sacred Nine out in old Peoria, and I was a holy terror on **third, now** I tell you. One day—"

But just at this **point in the** history it occurred to Rollo **to** send the **ball** over the plate. **Mr.** Holliday **saw it** coming; **he** shut both eyes and dodged for his life, but the ball hit his bat and went spinning straight up in the air. Thanny shouted " Foul!" ran under **it,** reached up, took it out of the atmosphere, **and** cried:

" Out!"

"Thanny," **said** his father sternly, " another **word and** you shall go straight **to bed!** If you do not improve **in** your habit of language I will send you to the reform school. Now Rollo," he continued, kindly, " that was a great deal better; very much better. I hit that **ball** with almost no difficulty. You are learning. **But you** will learn more rapidly if you **do** not expend so much unnecessary

69

strength in throwing the ball. Once more, now, and gently; I do not wish you to injure your arm."

Rollo leaned forward and tossed the ball toward his father very gently indeed, much as his sister Mary would have done, only, of course, in a more direct line. Mr. Holliday's eyes lit up with their old fire as he saw the on-coming sphere. He swept his bat around his head in a fierce semi-circle, caught the ball fair on the end of it, and sent it over Rollo's head, crashing into the kitchen window amid a jingle of glass and a crash of crockery, wild shrieks from the invisible maid servant and delighted howls from Rollo and Thanny of "Good boy!" "You own the town!" "All the way round!"

Mr. Holliday was a man whose nervous organism was so sensitive that he could not endure the lightest shock of excitement. The confusion and general uproar distracted him.

"Thanny!" he shouted, "go into the house! Go into the house and go right to bed!"

"Thanny," said Rollo, in a low tone,

70

. . . *His eyes lit up with the old fire as he saw the on-coming sphere. He swept his bat around his head in a fierce semi-circle.* (Page 70.)

"you're suspended; that's what you get for jollying the umpire."

"Rollo," said his father, "I will not have you quarreling with Thanny. I can correct him without your interference. And, besides, you have wrought enough mischief for one day. Just see what you have done with your careless throwing. You have broken the window, and I do not know how many things on the kitchen table. You careless, inattentive boy. I would do right if I should make you pay for all this damage out of your own pocket-money. And I would, if you had any. I may do so, nevertheless. And there is Jane, bathing her eye at the pump. You have probably put it out by your wild pitching. If she dies, I will make you wash the dishes until she returns. I thought all boys could throw straight naturally without any training. You discourage me. Now come here and take this bat, and I will show you how to pitch a ball without breaking all the glass in the township. And see if you can learn to bat any better than you can pitch."

Rollo took the bat, poised himself lightly, and kept up a gentle oscillation of the stick while he waited.

"Hold it still!" yelled his father, whose nerves were sorely shaken. "How can I pitch a ball to you when you keep flourishing that club like an anarchist in procession. Hold it still, I tell you!"

Rollo dropped the bat to an easy slant over his shoulder and looked attentively at his father. The ball came in. Rollo caught it right on the nose of the bat and sent it whizzing directly at the pitcher. Mr. Holliday held his hands straight out before him and spread his fingers.

"I've got her!" he shouted.

And then the ball hit his hands, scattered them, and passed on against his chest with a jolt that shook his system to its foundations. A melancholy howl rent the air as he doubled up and tried to rub his chest and knead all his fingers on both hands at the same time.

"Rollo," he gasped, "you go to bed too! Go to bed and stay there six weeks. And when you get up, put on one of your sister's dresses and play golf. You'll never learn to play ball if you practice a thousand years. I never saw such a boy. You have probably broken my lung. And I do not suppose I shall ever use my hands again. You can't play tiddle-de-winks. Oh dear, oh dear!''

Rollo sadly laid away the bat and the ball and went to bed, where he and Thanny sparred with pillows until tea time, when they were bailed out of prison by their mother. Mr. Holliday had recovered his good humor. His fingers were multifariously bandaged and he smelled of arnica like a drug store. But he was reminiscent and animated. He talked of the old times and the old days, and of Peoria and Hinman's, as was his wont oft as he felt boyish.

"And town ball," he said, "good old town ball! There was no limit to the number on a side. The ring was anywhere from three hundred feet to a mile in circumference, according to whether we played on a vacant Pingree lot or out on the open prairie. We tossed up a bat—wet or dry—for first choice, and then chose the whole school on the sides. The **bat** was **a board,** about the general shape of a **Roman** galley oar and not quite so wide as a **barn** door. The ball was **of solid** India rubber; a little fellow could hit **it a** hundred yards, and a big boy, **with a** hickory club, could **send it** clear over the **bluffs** or **across** the lake. We broke all **the** windows **in** the school-house **the** first day, and finished **up** every pane **of glass in the** neighborhood **before** the season **closed. The side that got its innings first** kept them until **school was out or the last boy** died. **Fun? Good game? Oh, boy of** these golden days, paying **fifty cents an hour for** the privilege of watching **a** lot of hired men do your playing for you—it beat two-old-cat."

SPELL **AND** DEFINE:

| Instruction | Miscalculation | Paralysis |
|---|---|---|
| Instantaneity | Pastime | Hasty |
| Liniment | Contusion | Supererogation |

**Can a boy** learn anything without **a** teacher?—Does the pupil ever know **more** than the instructor?—And why not?—How long does it require one to learn to speak and write the Spanish language correctly in six easy les-

sons, at home, without a master?—And in how many
lessons can one be taught to walk Spanish?—What is
meant by "a rooter"?—What is the difference between
a "rooter" and a "fan"?—Parse "hoodoo."—What is
the philology of "crank"?—Describe a closely con-
tested game of "one-old-cat," with diagrams.—What
is meant by "a rank decision"?—Translate into collo-
quial English the phrase, "Good eye Bill!"—Put into
bleaching board Latin, "Rotten umpire."—Why is he
so-called?

# ROLLO LEARNING TO TRAVEL

## VI

OLLO had never been very far away from home. So one morning, when Mr. Holliday had business in town, he said to Rollo:

"Rollo, there is nothing which rounds out one's education so gracefully, which so symmetrically broadens one's ideas, gives such catholicity to the mind, so completely eradicates petty conceit and narrow egotism, as travel. Providing, always, that the man has some sense, not much, but just a little bit, before he sets out on his travels. If he be a fool, however, traveling only aggravates his complaint. A wise man, who had a great deal to do with fools, once wrote,

' Though thou shouldst **bray a** fool **in a** mortar among wheat with **a** pestle, **yet** will **not** his foolishness depart from him.' And this **is** true. **He** would still be a fool; pulverized, indeed, but all there; just as much fool as ever. Worse, indeed; he would be **a** pestilent fool.''

**And Mr.** Holliday smiled **grimly,** but **not** unkindly, **at** his **little** joke. **Then he** continued:

''**Now**, my son, if you will be a good boy this morning, and saw up **a** lot of nice green limb-wood for your mother—for this is baking day—and clean up the back yard, **and** cut the grass **on the** lawn, **and** lead the horse **over to** the blacksmith shop and tell Mr. Slaketroff that he has **put** the hind shoes **on** the fore feet and **I** want them changed, **and** then hurry back and whitewash the hen house, and get yourself nicely washed and dressed by noon, you **may** go to the village with me.''

Rollo clapped his hands with delight, and said **he** would **be** ready to go **by** eleven o'clock.

**77**

Rollo then proceeded to bribe Thanny, principally with promises, to assist him with his morning's chores. Thanny, who had quite a commercial mind, accepted these promissory notes at large discount, having learned that business men were in the habit of exaggerating the discount in proportion to the promisor's necessities. Rollo explained to Thanny that by cutting the limb-wood an inch too long for the stove it would last longer. But Thanny, whose shoulders were really quite sore, and whose back gave him considerable pain, said that he had reformed, and was not going to play hookey, nor cheat about anything any more.

Rollo said that was right. He said he sometimes thought it was a pity that the pain from a licking did not last longer. He said that everybody in the world would probably join the church and be good, if they didn't get over headaches and backaches so soon. If some man would invent a gad with which you could hit a boy a lick on the first of January that would smart until the end of December, everybody in the world would be as orderly and well-behaved and regular in their hours and meals, and as steady at their work, as the convicts in a well conducted penitentiary. This was quite large talk from Rollo, but it was the result of constant association with his father.

Thanny's teacher had had a long talk with him on the previous evening upon the subject of truancy. She was a very winsome woman, bright and sparkling, and when Thanny gave her some "back talk," as he called it, she seized a rattan with a grip that turned her knuckles white, and counted all the stitches in the back seams of Thanny's jacket with it. The stitches held, because Thanny's mother did her own sewing. But the rattan looked tired for a week. The following morning Mr. Holliday inspected the teacher's work by the same method. And this was why Thanny was feeling superhumanly virtuous, because he had just parted from his father when Rollo approached him.

Sure enough, Rollo was quite ready to go with his father early in the afternoon. Indeed he was ready before his father was. As they drove out the gate Mr. Holliday said:

"Did you get all your tasks completed, Rollo?"

To which Rollo replied, being deeply impressed with Thanny's lecture:

"Not quite, sir."

This answer appeared to satisfy Mr. Holliday, and it gave Rollo a very broad margin. Indeed, Mr. Holliday discovered, the following morning, that the margin ran clear across the woof of the job into the selvedge.

They drove to the station in the Germantown, an indestructible vehicle which was invented in Pennsylvania several thousand years before the flood. None have been made since, although there are over a million in use. The Germantown is a wagon modeled after and in the livery of the Black Maria, in which anything from a picnic party to a siege gun can be hauled. It is somewhat less cheerful in appearance than a hearse, although not quite so heavy, however, as the old New England carry-all, of which it is probably a sport—that is, **if it be not** sacrilege to speak **of** such a combination as a sport.

**Mr.** Holliday was a Puritan. His fathers came over with the Pilgrims. **Of** course, no Hollidays **were** allowed on the Mayflower, but **Mr.** Holliday's great-grandfather registered himself **as** Fast-day, **and** came through **all** right. The keenest expert could **not** detect any difference between **the** Massachusetts Fast Day, recently deceased—died of jimjams, probably—and the wildest holiday that **ever** romped around as Christmas **in Mexico or** as the fourth of July in Arizona.

Rollo asked permission to **drive,** but his **father said "No;** the **horse** might bolt and **run away, and the** carriage **would be** broken and they **might be** killed." **As** Rollo had once seen a **broken** anvil, **he did not doubt** that some terrific convulsion **of** nature might strain one of the weaker parts **of a German-**town. His father said that he had to drive Cotton Mather—that was the name **of the** horse—with **a** tight rein and **a** firm wrist, for **he was very** high-spirited. Cotton Mather was 110 years **old.** When he was **a** colt, **of**

81

course, he **was** older than that. His neck, which was **very** long and flexible, fitted at the smaller end into the middle of his head; the large end, which was made **for the** collar, grew into his body.

When they had traveled for quite **a** long distance out into the world, which lies all around Bryn Mawr, and even projects **a** little ways into it—between Easter Sunday and Carnival—Rollo's father allowed Rollo to take the reins, saying that he would watch him and teach him to drive. **Rollo** was very proud, **albeit a** trifle nervous. Presently they came **to a** cross-road, which is a place in the country at which anywhere from two **to** seven roads meet and cross at different angles, acute, obtuse, right, salient and re-entrant. At one side of the crossing, far away from the focus, a finger-board, or guide-post, is set up **by the** supervisors. The finger-board **is** nailed high upon the post. The name **of** the town indicated, **and** the number of miles is painted **in** small letters, in gray paint on a drab ground, so that it is extremely difficult to read. But **at** the **end of** the board the letter ''M,''

*Rollo's father allowed Rollo to take the reins, saying he would watch him and teach him to drive. Rollo was very proud. (Page 82.)*

standing for miles, is painted bold, black and large. Thus, the average finger-board presents this appearance to the traveler:

"Why are the guide-boards painted so dimly?" asked Rollo.

"Because there is no reason for it," replied his father, "that is why It is one of the traditions of the office to make them in this way."

"And do I turn down this road to the left, the way the finger-board points, to go to Kickapoo Town?" asked Rollo.

"No," replied his father, "you go in exactly the opposite direction. That is another tradition of the office. You see, my son, the guide-boards are set up after this manner. The finger-board is nailed to the post in the shop, which is the barn of the supervisor. They are then loaded into a wagon and sent out on the road in charge of a man who can not read. He is instructed to set a post at every road crossing, which he does, setting the post firmly and making a good job of it, without any reference to the direction in which the boards point. In this way the traveler is more easily confused; he gets hopelessly lost, and drives through more toll-gates, and pays more money into the coffers of the benevolent society which controls the roads in the interest of the wagon and repair shops. Now, at this cross-road we turn to the right; pull on the right hand line."

Rollo hastily began to pull in the slack, hand over hand, and as he coiled it neatly away he was surprised to see Cotton Mather's head turning around and coming slowly after it, until his solemn face was staring at the occupants of the Germantown.

" Pull away," cried Mr. Holliday—" Haul hard to wind'ard! Bring him around!"

"But," said Rollo, "I am afraid I will pull his head off!"

" No, you won't," replied his father, " keep on pulling, he'll begin to turn by and by."

And so, indeed, he did. Cotton Mather had a habit, when the driver put him on another tack, of turning his head around after the drawing line as far as he could, while he continued to move straight forward on the old course. Uncle George said he was a good horse before the wind, but he hung in stays. However, he finally drifted around all right, and got under way again, picking up his feet, one after another, very soon after putting them down, in regular alternation, and moving them to locations on the ground somewhat further forward. In this way they made considerable progress. Rollo's father explained to him, that if the horse did not move his feet in this manner, but allowed them to remain where he deposited them, he would stand still, and they would not get anywhere.

"Wherefore, my son," he continued, "while it is a good thing for a man to put his foot down, and we often hear him commended for so doing, it is quite certain that the man who never does any thing else will never go anywhere. It is quite important in making progress to pick your foot up and place it in advance of the other, and keep on doing this. I once knew a man who prided himself greatly because he had acquired a reputation for putting his foot down. People foolishly or with guile, I know not—praised him for it. And he kept on doing it. But one morning, after doing this for about fifty years, he woke up and discovered that the world had been moving all this time, and that his generation, fifty years beyond him, simply looked over its shoulder whenever they heard him put his foot down with a new stamp in the same old place, laughed, and went on. When you hear of a man whose sole reputation is that he is a chronic ' objector,' do not waste any time or turn out of your way to go and see him. You can find him right there, in the same place, any time during your life, and you can see him at your leisure. He won't go away.''

In this manner did Mr. Holliday impart useful information to his little son on their journeys. And Rollo being very attentive, and eager to acquire knowledge, never forgot any

thing which he remembered. **He** now interrupted his father to say:

" We are coming to the railroad crossing."

" **I am very** glad that you are so observ-
ing, my son," said Mr. Holliday. " Your
great-uncle, Winthrop Emerson Beenes, lost
his life at such a crossing as this by reason **of**
his studious and abstracted habit **of** mind.
**He was a** graduate of the Universal University
**of all** universal universities, having completed
**the** entire course of four years in one summer
by correspondence, receiving a diploma which
**cost** him fifty dollars, including the frame.
This gave him a hunger for intellectual pabu-
**lum** which **he** could **not** satisfy. **One summer morning he was** driving to the **city** with
a jag **of wood, when,** approaching **a** railway
crossing, **he** observed **a** new sign in position.
Stopping his team midway **on** the rails where
he could get a good view, he began to read,
after his own deliberate **and** painstaking
method:

" R-a-i-l—rail, r-o-a-d, road, railroad—
**c-r-o-s, cros, s-i-n-g,** sing, crossing, railroad
crossing; **l-o, double o-k,** look; railroad

crossing; look; o-u-t, out, railroad crossing; look out; f-o-r, for—railroad crossing; look out for—t-h-e, the—railroad crossing; look out for the—.''

"And just then the limited express came thundering along and filled the air with buckles, and bits of harness, and horse-shoes, and pieces of wagon, and fragments of wood, and the greater portion of your great-uncle Winthrop. He lived only long enough, after his return to earth, to say that he would die happy if he only knew what it was he was to look out for.''

" One should be very careful, then,'' said Rollo, " when crossing the railroad tracks? ''

" It is not a railroad,'' replied his father, " it is a railway. What you call the tracks are not the tracks, but the line. And the rails are not the rails, but the metals. The yard engine is a shifting engine; the switch is a siding; we do not switch cars, we shunt them; the conductor is not the conductor, but the guard; the engineer is the driver; the fireman is the stoker; the ties are sleepers; the passenger car is a coach; the baggage is the luggage van, and the baggage checks **are** the brawsses."

" But why are **all** these things other than what they are?" asked Rollo.

" Because **it is** English," replied **his** father.

" But," said Rollo, " **the** Hottentots probably have names **for** these things still **more** foreign. Why **not use the names they** would give them?"

" I presume it would answer quite as well," replied his **father,** "any thing would be proper, so **it be** not American. I merely wish **you to avoid** the vernacular **of your** native country."

"**And** one **thing,**" said his father in **conclusion,** " wherever you go **in your travels, I** beg you to remember."

" What is that?" asked Rollo.

" Remember the waiter," said his **father,** with a hollow lawff.

| Tip | Tip | **Tip** |
|-----|-----|---------|
| Tip | **Tip** | **Tip** |
| Tip | **Tip** | **Tip** |

Which is the oldest railroad in the United States ?
—And which is the worst ?—That is correct. And
which is the meanest ?—Yes ; that is correct. And
which is, in all respects, the best ?—State how long,
giving the answer in years, you have had a pass over
that road.—Describe the habits of a railway hog.—If a
man habitually sits on a bench at home, eats pie with
a knife, and wipes his fingers on his hair, how many
seats will he occupy in a railway car ?—A boy at home
is thirteen years old, and weighs 108 pounds ; how old
will he be when his mother takes him out to Mahaha
to see grandpa ?—Correct ; and how does he lose the
seven years ?—A baggage man weighing 210 pounds
sits on a ninety pound trunk while he weighs it ; how
much is the " excess baggage " ?

## VII

ONE evening near the latter end of the same day of the week, Rollo came home from school a few hours behind time, but making good steam and running fast. He saw his mother standing under the honeysuckle vines that bowered the piazza, but instead of hastening straight to her, as usual, he steered himself in the direction of the woodshed, expressing his intention, as he passed Jane at the kitchen window, of preparing enough kindling wood to last until the following Christmas.

A boy never loses this disposition to be superfluously useful and voluntarily obliging,

91

after he has committed transgression, until he has safely passed his ninety-second year. After that time he is as liable to be self-assertive and impudent as a boy who has just broken a window is sure to be polite and respectful.

His mother hailed him twice before he wanted to hear, but her voice came floating softly into his heart, and the little boy's habit of obedience asserted itself as he dropped the hatchet and slowly rounded to in quarantine.

"Rollo, dear," his mother said, "how came you to be so late?"

"'Taint late," Rollo said, "I run all the way from school fast as I could. Didn't you see me run down the path?"

"But," his mother said, "school closes at three o'clock, and it is now half past six; how does that come?"

"Oh, yes," replied Rollo, rather too cheerfully for the occasion. "I know now; got kep' in. Missed my jography lesson."

"I think my little boy has missed a lesson," his mother said, gently, "but it wasn't in one of his school-books. Why are you so late, Rollo? Where have you been since school closed?''

"Oh!" said Rollo, with an air of sudden recollection. "I forgot; had to go home with a sick boy. He pushed a bean up his nose so far he couldn't get it back again. Mighty sick. His folks think mebbe he'll die."

And Rollo looked very sad as he thought of it. His eyes were bent upon his bare feet, as with prehensile toes he scraped a little fort in the dust of the path. It was a pathetic picture; the dying boy with one barrel of his nose loaded with a single bean, slowly passing away from life with all its cares, its disappointing experiments in nasal agriculture, so often resulting in naught but weariness of flesh and vexation of spirit; his weeping friends grouped about the bed, vainly imploring him to make one more effort to transform his nose into a catapult, firing a common pole-bean (*Phaseolus vulgaris*) into space at short range—small wonder that Rollo's heart sank as he reviewed the incident which never occurred.

"Rollo," his mother said, without commenting upon the tragedy, "your teacher was here an hour ago, and said you had not been in school this afternoon. How did that happen, Rollo?"

"Forgot," said Rollo, "thought all the time it was Saturday. It was yesterday I got kep' in."

"Rollo," said his mother, "look at me. Didn't you go off with the boys and go in swimming this afternoon?"

Rollo tried hard to look at his mother. But all the beans that never went up all the noses that never were seemed loaded upon his head. He couldn't tell what made it so heavy. Look into his mother's face! Why, there was nothing else in all this world of beauty at which he loved so well to look. But somehow his head would not come up. He added a strong bastion to the little fortress in the dust, as though it might strengthen his position. But he only said:

" Nome."

**And** his voice sounded **so** strange and harsh that he looked around guiltily, as though **half** expecting to see Gub Smoucher, the meanest boy in school, standing there, saying it over **his** shoulder.

" **Don't** look **down at your** feet, Rollo," his mother said, and **it** seemed to him **he** never heard **her** speak so gently, " look into **my** face, just while you answer **me**. Weren't you down at **the** creek this afternoon? "

Rollo did try once more, but there was only **one** thing **in** the world that was heavier than **the** heavy head that hung upon his drooping shoulders. And that was the heart **of a** frightened **boy** beating like **a** great triphammer, **as** though **it** would pound its way through **the** walls **of** his breast, **and show** itself and all **its** thoughts and secrets, in spite of the lying lips that were trying so hard to hide them. Rollo strengthened the redoubt a little, and **made the** parapet higher, before **he** answered,

" Nope."

" But your hair is all wet, my son," his mother said.

" Yes, I know," replied Rollo; " that's sweat. Run so fast to get home on time; that's what made that."

"And your shirt is on wrong side out," said his mother.

" Yes," Rollo said, " I knowed that. Put it on that way on purpose this morning. For luck. Always win when you play keeps if your shirt is wrong side out."

" But one sleeve of your shirt is not on your arm at all," his mother said, " and there is a knot tied in it. How did that happen? "

" Why," Rollo said, " Tobe Wilkerson done that when I wasn't lookin'."

" But what were you doing with your shirt off, Rollo? "

Rollo constructed a' lunette in front of his fort very slowly, for his stronghold was being sorely pressed by the besiegers. By and by he said:

" I didn't have it off at all. Tobe just

96

took and tied that knot in when I had it on.
That's just what he done. And I didn't
know it. He tied it in school. 'Deed an'
double, he did!''

"Tell the truth, Rollo, dear; tell your
mother."

Rollo planned a subterranean way of escape from his beleaguered citadel, for it
seemed to him the lines were being drawn
very closely about him, and he feared the
time for the final assault was not very far
away. He made another effort to lift his
face, but his glances were glued to the
ground. His eyes were in the dust.

"Honest Injun, ma, he did; honor bri—"

But somehow his voice, which started out
brave and strong with "honest Injun," faltered and quavered away into a tremulous
whisper when it tried to say "honor bright,"
like a good soldier forced into the enemy's
uniform to fight under a flag he despises.
His nervous toes hastily completed the line
of retreat from a stronghold that was turning
into a trap.

7                97

"My little boy," his **mother** said, very gently and softly.

**As** she spoke Rollo made one mighty struggle, and this time he did manage to lift his blue eyes until they looked into his moth**er's** brown ones, straight as a ray of sunshine. And then, he only saw her for just a little moment. **For a** great mist of tears came drifting between his eyes and her dear face, like a fog-bank coming up out **of the** sea. And that **was all.**

**Because, now that** he **could not see** her— **though but a minute** ago **he** wished he might **not—the** world seemed so big, and lonely, and **dark to** him—though just now he wanted some dark place in which to hide from her— that he reached out his arms to see if she were still there. As he touched her, **as he** sprang forward and clung **to her, he set** his **foot on** the little fortress in **the dust and** crushed **all his** poor, weak refuge **of** lies— **its** mean little hiding places, all its frail bombproofs, and its treacherous sally ports into the dust of which it was builded. He clung to

. . . . At last the broken sobs and the low singing blended softly together, then ceased; the sun went down and the twilight came creeping silently into the room. (Page 94.)

her as though he would never, never let go of
her again in all his life. His head had found
its old pillow—never so soft, and sweet, and
safe as now. Her arms were about his neck,
hiding her little boy's face from everybody
but herself. Even the rebellious little scalp-
lock, that he could never brush down, looked
pathetic as it drooped in its place like a de-
jected plume.

She did not say much; Rollo's mother
was one of those rare teachers—who know
when silence is the wisest and sweetest
monitor and comforter in this garrulous
old world. She led the little boy into the
sitting-room and sat down with him nestled
in her arms, and sung the old cradle songs
over him just as she used to do. And
Rollo's crying grew fainter, until at last the
broken sobs and the low singing blended
softly together, then ceased; the sun went
down and the twilight came creeping silently
into the room.

When Rollo's father came home the
lamps were not lighted; a great silver
star, hanging in the rosy west, was look-

ing in at the window, and there in the twilight and starlight Rollo's mother sat rocking, and the great big boy, with the tear stains on his grimy face, lay fast asleep in his mother's arms. And Mr. Holliday knew there had been trouble and good medicine for it. So he stooped to kiss the little dusty face very gently, and thought, as he tip-toed out of the room, that, after all, Rollo's mother was right when she said that men who had once been babies never got entirely over it, but were babies a little bit, when in pain or trouble, all the days of their life.

But they don't have their mothers to go to all their lives. And that's a good thing for a boy to remember before he forgets it.

This wasn't the last time Rollo got into trouble. Because trouble is a plant that is indigenous to the soil of this planet, so that it grows all the way along the road from the slough of Despond to the land of Beulah, on both sides of the path, thick as alders on a trout brook, tangled as dewberry vines, and vicious as poison ivy. So it happened that Rollo got into trouble once afterward, and the next time; **and another** time; **and the time** after that; and then again; **and all the** other times. And long after his **old** pillow **had been taken** away from **his** head, when **he had** learned **to** go **to** another comforter, **often as** trouble or sorrow came **into** his life, **he** recalled that quiet evening **in his** old home; **with** the daylight fading **into twilight and** the stars lighting the twilight **out of** the world; **he** could hear her voice singing the cradle songs again, and he loved **to** read in the Book of Consolation—

"**As** one whom his mother comforteth, so **will I** comfort you."

**So Rollo,** crying himself **to** sleep **in his** mother**'s arms,** was learning one of the hardest lessons **in all** this great kindergarten— " How Not **To.**"

SPELL AND **DEFINE:**

| | | |
|---|---|---|
| Erasure | Blot | Retrograde |
| Misfit | Derailment | Politics |
| Countermarch | Effacement | Dissimulation |

**Construe** " *Facilis descensus averni.*"—What is the **fare to Nevada** ?—Which **is easier** for a flying machine

101

—to fly up or fly down?—And why?—Why, then, is it so much easier to lay down a promissory note than **to take it up**?—Give **an** example.—How long did it **take Adam to** get **out of the** Garden of Eden?—And how long has it taken his family to get back?

## VIII

OME time after the oc-
currences which happened
previously, **Mr.** Holliday
came home from the **vil-**
lage rather unexpectedly,
**and** walked around to **the**
wood-shed to see how Rollo was coming on
with the tale of winter stove-wood. Rollo had
some misgivings about this contract himself.
Indeed, when it was advertised to let, he hesi-
tated about putting in a bid on it, and only was
induced to **do so by** his father's arguments **and**
**by** his promise to assist him in any serious crisis.
He said **at** any time when he **perceived** that
Rollo was falling behind with the delivery of
short sticks every Saturday evening, he would
call him up at five o'clock Monday morning,

and at four o'clock Tuesday, and if he still failed to bring his contract up to the stated figure, at three on Wednesday, and so on. He said he was not the man to stand around and let a boy lose money on a good contract by loss of time, when he could just as well as not work him in a couple or three hours extra every day.

"Time is money," concluded Mr. Holliday, "and many a boy loses a good job by not being around when his father wants him."

Saying which, Mr. Holliday went to the mirror and carefully examined his throat, which was quite raw and inflamed, having been overworked the preceding afternoon, when he had called, and shouted, and yelled for Rollo and Thanny from two o'clock till three, to come to the barn and turn the grindstone a little, while he put a razor-edge on two axes, a hatchet, a weed-scythe, a couple of stalk-cutters, the butcher-knife, the bread-knife, a cradle-blade, the broad-ax and a few chisels.

Rollo and Thanny were down at the creek fishing at the time their father wanted boy-power on the grindstone. They heard the shouting, but they thought it was their neighbor, old Mr. Thistlepod, drowning in the swimming hole. They said they wanted to go to his assistance, and would have done so, gladly, but for the fear that his bull-dog, Turk Thistlepod, was with him, and would tear them limb from limb. They said they had observed that the dog was always untied when they went past the orchard, consequently they supposed he was loose all the time. Frequently they had gone past the orchard at different times of the day and late in the evening—sometimes as late as half past nine o'clock in the afternoon—on purpose to see if the dog was shut up. But no; he was always tied loose; always prowling about in a mean, suspicious manner, and always he growled in a threatening tone if they just stood on the lower rail of the fence to see more clearly. They told their Uncle George about it, and he said they were *personæ non grati* with that dog and had better suspend all diplomatic relations with him.

The two boys felt very sad, they said, as

they thought of **old Mr.** Thistlepod struggling in the treacherous element, and slowly
going down for the third time, which would
be " **out.** " But they could not help remembering that the dog had always shown a **most**
unreasonable antipathy to them, and they
feared it might be extremely difficult to over-
come his prejudice at a moment's notice.

You couldn't rescue a drowning man, Rollo
said, **and** pacify **an** excited bull-dog **at** the
same time, without more **or** less neglecting
**one branch of the** business. And beside,
Thanny **had on his Sunday** pantaloons, his
**others being in** the shops getting a new dome
put in, **so** that whether he jumped into the
water, or the dog jumped into him, the
ruin of his best apparel was inevitable if they
attempted **a** rescue.

**Rollo** and Thanny were growing **to be very**
thoughtful **boys.** Their father said that sometimes he feared they thought **too much** and
**too** far ahead in some matters.

But Rollo said **no; he** used **to do that**
when he was younger. But he had reformed.
" Because, papa," he said, " you may **re-**

member that on several occasions, when you came home in the evening, you called me into your study and said, ' Rollo, what is this which I hear about you to-day?' And several times, desiring to save the time and expense of a trial, and being naturally frank with you, I owned up at once and told you, to the best of my ability, what it was. But now and then I owned up to the wrong thing—something which you hadn't heard about. And then I was in for two of them. So that now, you may have observed, I never plead until I hear the indictment read.''

Rollo added that this was safer, because you never could tell what was going to happen next in their family, but Thanny said that didn't bother him so much as to be put in the witness-box unexpectedly, and then not be able to remember clearly what had happened last.

And as he said that, Rollo gave a sudden little gasp, for he just remembered that Mr. Thistlepod's bull-dog had bitten Jonas last week, and had gone into a decline the day following, and **before** Saturday night had **died** of inflammatory tuberculosis aggravated **by** symptoms of malignant strychninism in the **other** lung.

Jonas was Mr. Holliday's **hired boy.**

One day, the other summer, when **Mr.** Holliday **and** Rollo were out driving, the horse, Cotton Mather, drifted so far to leeward (pronounced lewrd), in making a turn on a hill road, tha**t** he **broke a trace and** began to back rapidly down **the** hill. **Mr.** Holliday shouted, "Whoa!" and Rollo **cried,** "Get **up!"** loudly and rapidly, but Cotton Mather **found it more** agreeable to follow the wagon down hill, and continued **so to** do with **a** steady acceleration of speed. **As** they thus retrograded down the incline, a boy sitting on a log at the roadside called out, apparently to nobody:

"Git on to de trolley!"

"Put a stone behind the wheel!" **shouted** Mr. Holliday, for **it** was he.

"**Fur a** nickel **I** will!" replied the **boy,** politely. **He** was poorly, but not ostentatiously dressed, and appeared to be very obliging.

Mr. Holliday said that he would give him a nickel as soon as the bank opened. The boy then picked up a large fragment of glacial drift and "chocked" the hind wheel with it, causing Cotton Mather to stop so abruptly that it stiffened his neck.

When they got out of the wagon to repair damages, Mr. Holliday asked the boy if he had a bit of twine about his person. The boy replied that he was long on string, and drew from one of his pockets a coil of fish-line, a piece of manilla rope, several small clusters of binding-twine, a loop of picture-wire, a bunch of rubber bands, a skein of black carpet thread, a guitar string, a spool of white cotton, three leather shoe strings, a couple of waxed ends, with bristles on them, and a small dog chain.

"Bid on anything you want, governor," said the boy, respectfully.

Mr. Holliday kindly took the entire assortment, saying, thoughtfully, that if he couldn't use all the outfit now it might come in handy some other time. **He** also informed the boy that **if he** killed his pigs before Christmas he **would pay** him next June, if the weather held **on and** the roads kept **up.**

The boy took off his hat and thanked him, saying that would suit him exactly; and as **he** was in no hurry he would just **go** home with the gentleman and wait for it.

And in this way Jonas, for that **was** the boy**'s** other name, became Mr. Holliday's hired **boy. He was a very** useful **boy,** and **taught Rollo and Thanny a** great many things. **He was very** obliging, **too,** and **never considered it a** hardship to quit work at **any time on a hot** day and go in swimming **with** the boys. He had to go swimming, he said, for his paralysis. It used to come on him while **he** was at work. Sometimes, while weeding **the** garden, he **would be paralyzed in** both **legs and one arm.** Then hearing **Rollo** whistle **over by** the **woods,** he **would look up and see** him **on the fence,** holding **up** his right **hand** with the first **and** second fingers spread apart. At this signal Jonas would drop his hoe, bound out of the garden like a rabbit, **jump over** the fence like a deer, **run** to beat Nancy Hanks for half a mile, leap into the swimming hole and splash around in **the** healing water until it was time **to** make his toilet and go after the cows.

Jonas' summer toilet consisted **of** three pieces; a pair of over-alls big enough **to** go around him twice; **a** hickory shirt, and one suspender **of** the same. Consequently he did **not** waste his time before the mirror. He was very systematic for **a** hired boy, and **knew** exactly how long it took **him to make** his toilet, **or** unmake it. When **he** went swimming it took him two and one-half seconds to **kick** himself out **of** his wardrobe, and about fifteen **to dress.** When he was called up in the morning, **it required** twenty-five **minutes** for him to arrange the three pieces **of his** apparel properly. This was his summer schedule. In the winter time, of course, **it** took longer.

There are very few boys like Jonas left in this **world.** He was a boy of intense vitality, **with** remarkable recuperative powers. Out **in the** field, while " raking after " **in** oats harvest, he would have sunstroke about eleven o'clock in the forenoon, and stagger feebly to the house, groping his way like a blind man, not expecting to live until he could get into the shade of the porch. But in about an hour, when the horn blew for dinner, he would be first at the table, get helped twice before the men could come in from the field, keep up with them all the time they were eating, and be ready to go out a-field with them and have a stroke of paralysis at half past three in the afternoon.

Paralysis and sunstroke were his summer afflictions. In the winter he had heart failures. When these attacks came on, he fell from his seat in school and had to be sent home on a passing sled.

Mr. Holliday sent Jonas to school three months every year. He wanted to send him five, but one teacher died and her successor struck. So Jonas went to Fairview school three months in the year, and learned more than all the rest of the boys did in six.

It was from Jonas that Mr. Thistlepod's bull dog contracted the malady of which he died. **One** evening Jonas was walking past **Mr.** Thistlepod's orchard in the gloaming. He had a sack **of** seed corn on his shoulder and **a** pan full **of** Lima beans in his hand. **He** was whistling between his teeth **in a** peculiarly shrill and irritating manner, when the dog ran up behind him **and bit** him in the bare leg. Jonas **gave a** mighty yell **and** let the sack **of seed corn** fall **on the** dog, thus pinning him to the earth while **the** boy made his escape. **Jonas** went home, put **a chew of** tobacco on the wound, over which he tied a piece **of ham** rind, some bruised plantain leaves **and a** mullein poultice, and then made his will. **He** did **not,** however, immediately give **away any of** the things **of** which **he** stood possessed, greatly to **the** disappointment **of** Rollo and Thanny. Jonas **said he** might not die **for a** great many years, but when he did die it would be because **of** that bite.

**The** third morning after the biting, however, word came to the Holliday place that the bull dog had gone into a decline. He must **have** gone into **it** during the night, be-

8          113

cause in the morning, when the family at Thistlepod Terrace first noticed him, he was lying on his back, quite unconscious; his legs were sticking straight up in the air, and his body was swollen to about five times its normal size. This, Jonas said, was a sure sign of lung disease. When they took the dog's temperature it was, as near as they could estimate, about forty-two degrees below zero. Then they gave up all hope, especially when the anemometer indicated that his respiration was merely nominal.

There was no formal announcement made of the dog's decease, old Mr. Thistlepod simply sending word to Jonas that if he ever caught him anywhere on his farm he would break every bone in his lazy carcass. When this was told Jonas, he explained to Rollo and Thanny that it was because old Mr. Thistlepod feared that Jonas would go mad and bite him if he went anywhere nigh to where he had himself been bitten.

The night after Turk's demise, Thanny was very ill with cholera morbus, and the doctor, who was sent for at 2 o'clock in the morning, said it was too early in the summer for him to eat so many apples; they looked nice, he said, but they were not sufficiently ripe to eat in quantities of one-half peck and upwards.

Thanny said he had eaten but two, and they were small ones, very mellow and quite ripe, with all the seeds jet black.

But doctor Goodpill said he had doctored boys long before Thanny's father was born, and in the course of his practice had probably prescribed for 284,000 cases of cholera morbus, hence he always made his diagnosis without any reference to the statements of the patient. So saying he gave Thanny a dose which made him wish he had eaten one more apple and died in the orchard.

### SPELL AND DEFINE:

| | | |
|---|---|---|
| Prudence | Miscellany | Dude |
| Dogwood-bark | Jimber-jawed | Gallus |
| Meat-hound | Hydrophobophobia | Job |

A boy eleven years old and three feet and five inches in height has a trousers pocket eighteen inches in circumference and four feet deep; how long will it take him to fill it?—Give an example.—Where would he put his other things?—Are dogs fond of green ap-

115

ples ?—And is this why they are so often found prowling about their **owners' orchards ?—Yes ; and which
would you** rather prefer, **a bite of hard, gnarly green
apple, or a bite** of dog **?—And why ?—Draw on the
board a** diagram of a boy spending a **June afternoon in
an October** orchard, before and after.—Name **one.—
What not infrequently happens** to a dog when **he
bites the wrong boy ?**

# ROLLO LEARNING TO LEARN

## IX

ANY other useful things did Rollo learn from constant and loving association with that good and wise man, his father. Because, however priggish and pompous, however shallow and stupid, Mr. Holliday might seem, in the judgment of his neighbors, to Rollo he was ever the wisest teacher, the best companion, the merriest playmate, the truest comrade to be found among men, and to this opinion Rollo clung most loyally long after other boys began to call him " grandpa," and tease him for stories about what he did when he was a boy. So Rollo and his father went to school

together, so long as they lived, and when Mr.
Holliday was graduated from this old kindergarten and went up into the high school, and
Rollo remained at his desk, all the years as
they came and went found him at the same
old lessons. They were a little harder after
his father got his degree and went out.

He missed the old teacher who studied by
his side; who was disciplined for his faults,
as Rollo was; who smarted for his mistakes,
as Rollo did; who blundered over his books,
as Rollo did; and who cried over the hard
places, as Rollo did; and who, better than
any other man in all this wide world, knew
how to get under Rollo's burdens; who knew,
as no other man in the world did, how to find
a way through the thickets and out of the
brambles; how to whitewash a path so that
Rollo could see it in the dark; who knew, in
this tangled old wilderness, just where to find
the healing herb of grace that always grows
not far away from the poison ivy; who knew
that a gnat is more irritating than a tiger, and
that mosquitoes worry more people, a million
times told, than do the lions; that mole-hills

disfigure more **lawns** than mountains, **and** so understood how to enter into the **little boy's** big troubles. **All** these things are also good things for Rollo's father to bear in mind while **he** is forgetting them, because they mean so much **to** Rollo.

So Rollo kept **on** learning **so** long as he lived; learning and unlearning, **which is much** the same thing, only harder. **A boy of** eighteen or nineteen is liable **to know a** great deal more, and to know it more positively, than **a man** of eighty. No hoary-headed sage, whose long and studious years have **been** passed **in** the study **of** books and things **and men,** ever **knows so** many things quite so positively **as a boy. But, if the boy** lives long enough, **and keeps on** learning, he **has** time to get rid **of a** great deal **of** his **youthful** knowledge. It hurts, oh yes. Pulling eyeteeth and triple-pronged molars is mirth-provoking pastime—summer-day ecstacy—compared with the pangs which accompany shredding off **great** solid slabs **and** layers of **wisdom that** sometimes press upon the young **man like** geological **strata. And** how does the youth get rid of all this superabundant knowledge? Oh, by a very simple process; he just keeps on airing it; and it disintegrates rapidly on exposure to the air.

"Time," says Ovid, "is the best doctor." And that is true. He amputates everything that is not a healthy appurtenance to his patient, and, last of all, he amputates the patient. So Rollo, learning and unlearning, all his days and some of his nights, soon learned that the sun got up early every day and went to bed late in the afternoon, just before twilight, and lasted longer than any man he ever knew who got up at noon and went to bed at 2 A. M. He learned it was best to ride when he couldn't fly, run when he couldn't ride, walk when he couldn't run, sit still when he couldn't get up, and saw wood or attend to his knitting all the time. He learned that there is the same pang in a broken toy and a broken heart, with a difference in degree only; that we make a resolution to break it, and break a record to make it; that it takes a hen to lay an egg and a friar to lay a ghost; that

the reason why the Sphinx kept a secret **for
three** thousand years is because she never had
one; that while only superstitious people **believe in** signs, wise people believe also **in**
cosines and tangents; that the best two-foot
rule is "never to kick **with** both feet **at**
once;" that the safe **side of a** stock deal **is**
the outside, and the man who gets taken **in**
is left out; that the preacher who collects **his**
own salary gets all the exercise he needs; that
the most **fatal** error **in diet is** never to eat
anything; that **a** fast life makes **a** torpid
liver; and that it is never too late to mend, because the **older a man** grows the **more re-
pairs he** needs.

So many, many things Rollo learned **in his**
three **score** years **and** ten **at** school that **he**
never could have remembered one-half **of**
them **if** he hadn't forgotten two-thirds **of**
them. And that which gave him the most
study was what to forget. Because it seemed
to the little boy, when his whiskers were
gray, that the things he wanted **to** forget, **which he** tried the hardest **and** most

faithfully to forget, remembered themselves; whereas the things which he tried most faithfully to remember blotted themselves out like snowflakes in August.

So hard it was for the little boy to learn how to remember; so much harder it was to learn how to forget. So much harder. He learned how to remember by and by. But he never forgot. And the things he remembered came drifting across the way of his pilgrimage late in the afternoon, a mellow sunshine that glorified everything it touched with the tender beauty of yesterday. And the things he could not forget came floating across the sky like clouds, and their shadows dropped into the sunshine of the memories. And the great love of the Heavenly Father made the picture beautiful with melting tenderness in spite of the shadows; maybe because of them. So much better God is to us than we are to ourselves.

So Rollo learned at last that the deeds of the morning are the dreams of the afternoon. He learned that when he was a little boy, and had learned to see, and hear, and play, and work, and rest; to believe, to suffer and to love, he had learned all that any one in this world could teach him, and that all his life long he was to go on learning these same things over and over and over.

NTIL at last, when he had learned all his lessons and school was out, somebody lifted him, just as they had done at the first. Darkened was the room, and quiet; now, as it had been then. Other people stood about him, very like the people who stood there on that other time.

There was a doctor now, as then; only this doctor wore a graver look, and carried a Book in his hand. There was a man's voice—the doctor's, strong and reassuring. There was a woman's voice, low and comforting.

The mother voice had passed into silence. But that was yet the one he could most distinctly hear. The others he heard, as he heard voices like them years ago. He could not then understand what they said; he did not understand them now.

He parted his lips again, but all his school-acquired wealth of many-syllabled eloquence, all his clear, lucid phrasing, had gone back to the old inarticulate cry.

Somebody at his bedside wept. Tears now, as then. But now they were not tears from his eyes.

Then, some one, bending over him, had said, "He came from heaven." Now, someone, stooping above him, said, "He has gone to heaven." The blessed, unfalter-ing faith that welcomed him, now bade him Godspeed, just as loving and trusting as ever, one unchanging thing in this world of change.

So the baby had walked in a little circle, after all, as all men, lost in a great trackless wilderness, are said alway to do.

As it was written thousands of years ago— "The dove found no rest for the sole of her foot, and she returned unto him in the Ark."

He felt weary now, as he was tired then.

By and by, having then for the first time opened his eyes, now for the last time he closed them. And so, as one who in the gathering darkness retraces his steps by a half-remembered path, much in the same way as he had come into this world, he went out of it.

Silence.

Light.

## END OF " ROLLO."

# CHIMES FROM A JESTER'S BELLS
## STORIES AND SKETCHES

## X

S I looked out of my prison window that afternoon, I wondered if the sun ever helped to make a lovelier day. All the land, the sky and the clouds formed a picture framed by the window that was glorified by the painting of June. The lanes were fringed with fragrant hedges; star-eyed daisies peeped out of the fallow fields; daintier wild flowers nestled in the woods, pearls in the beds of velvet moss. Down in the meadows the buttercups gleamed like fallen stars. Over the low hills soft winds whispered to the rustling leaves of other summer days, long years gone by. Deep in the shadowy woods the little brook laughed and sung and babbled to itself like a child at play.

Here and there a home roof showed itself among the trees. The distant calls of children came rippling in at my window. The long road wound away, yellow and quiet, until it turned out of sight beyond the little church with its gray stone walls and white spire, slender and graceful.

And over all the picture lay the sense of peace. Not a harsh shadow; not a discordant note. Far away a brooding dove sobbed upon the silence, accenting the hush that lay upon the world with a touch of exquisite sorrow. A strain of song from a meadow lark, heard once, and no more. The mellow whistle of a robin, at broken intervals. These, with the laughter of the playing children, blessed the tranquillity of the afternoon. A beautiful world; a world at rest. The benediction of it all came even into my prison room.

Clear, mellow, distant, a ripple of bugle notes comes echoing into the quiet. My heart, as though it were a prisoner like myself, leaped and throbbed within the walls of my breast. I hasten to the window and look out with straining eyes. In the fluttering leaves that mask the hillside within my view I can discern no glitter of bayonets. I listen with eager intensity for the dull rumble of a battery wheeling into position. The notes of the bugle have fallen silent; no movement follows them.

And yet it is not quiet enough. The sighing of the wind irritates me; the rustling of the maple under my window frets me. I want the leaves and the brook to keep still while I listen for a stealthy footstep; the crackling of a twig; the muffled tramp of a column of men stealing through the woods under leafy cover. I listen for the shrill neigh of an excited horse; for a rhythmic clatter of hoof-beats; a sharp carbine shot ringing out into the stillness. Looking to right and left, far as my narrow window will let me look, I listen, ever since I heard the bugle call wind through the silence, for sterner music than the robin's song and the murmur of the little brook.

"March!"

At last! I can see nothing from this window of mine, this mere picture frame! The voice comes like an echo of the bugle—a boyish voice, softened by the distance. I picture to myself the fair-haired lieutenant who commands the skirmishers. He has blue eyes, I doubt not; and nerves of steel; these blue-eyed soldiers are calm, self-possessed fellows; good shots; undismayed by defeat, not exhilarated by triumph. Ah, those days made men of striplings; the school-boy fought beside the veteran; the adjutant of twenty rode with the colonel of forty-five.

Silence again. Will the line never come in sight? Where is the enemy? Where are my comrades?

" Halt! "

Again the silence. Now, once more the bugle thrills down the unseen line. I can hear the hurried tramp of feet; the terrible stealthiness of preparation. All about me the tide of battle will surge and beat, save where I might see it. I—penned in this cage on such a day and at such a time; chained to the work-bench, while shrilling bugle and clanking sabers call in notes that burn **into my** heart like words of fire, so well **do I** understand them. And I **am** here!

"March!"

Away **off** the flam, flam, flam, **of a drum,** cadencing the step **of** the moving column. Nearer it comes; **and** nearer; **now** it sweeps **away;** faints; throbs faintly into silence **again.**

Tramp, tramp, tramp. Muffled; distinct; stepping nearer with every footfall.

"There they come!" shouts some one. I **find it** hard to breathe in this pent-up excitement. I press my hand **on** my heart, and **wait for the** first shot on the skirmish line. **Surely they must see each** other soon!

"Ready!"

**The** click **of a** musket, sharp, keen; **like a** threat in cold blood! If the robin would only hush his song for a minute! I listen **for the** light, clear voice again. I wonder **if—**

"Fire!"

How the cheers, breaking up in waves **of** sound, drown the volleying crash of musketry! **Again the** light voice calls "Fire!"

Again the shrill cheers rise on the **air of** June, and yet again. **The** bugle breaks into them with **its** musical command. I hear the rat**tling** wheels as a battery is hurried forward into position. I hear a drum beating with excited haste. I hear the confusion of trampling feet, rushing here and there. Some one is calling loudly for " the flag!"

Once, so close to my prison does **the** angry rush of the *mêlée* come, I hear a saber spring **from** its scabbard **with an angry sweep.** And **all** this time, listening **to the** fierce orchestra of **war, I** can see only **the** peaceful setting **of** the **stage; the** golden sunshine; **the** fluttering leaves; **the** restless shadows, tired of play, lengthening into the waning afternoon, while now and again, floating into my window with the shouts and the bugle calls, drifts the mellow whistle of the robin.

The cheering grows fainter, **as** the shadows over meadow and hillside grow longer. The robin's vesper music ceases. Sweet and beautifully imperious the bugle sounds again. It is " the recall." **A** pall **of** silence falls **upon the** clamor **of** the battle. I try my prison door. It yields to my hand. I hasten down a stairway with swift and silent tread. I step through a curtained door and stand upon the field where the waves of contention had dashed and thundered.

The level rays of the setting sun rest pityingly upon the helpless, motionless figures stretched at my feet—the evening blessing upon the dead. Here, just before me, is the overturned cannon, with a shattered wheel. Stretched across its brazen muzzle is an artillery sergeant, his nerveless hand still grasping a broken saber. Not far from the gun, a group of infantry soldiers, lying as they fell in the charge. Never again will they stand before hostile gun or under friendly flag. I look down upon a trooper in brilliant uniform, dressed for a royal death—headless he lies under the horse that has fallen upon him.

A little drummer boy—how came he so far away from the mother's arms that will ache for the pressure of his head?—sleeps by his shattered drum, his broken hand resting white and stiff upon its torn head. Ghastly and horrible, here is a head, the blue cap with its bright pompon of white and scarlet still jauntily crowning the pallid brow. Here is a saber, bent and twisted in the fury and stress of the hand-to-hand struggle over the guns. I walk among the distorted bodies. Crippled horses lie prone on their sides, or with the dumb, uncomplaining patience of their kind, stand wearily waiting for weakness to cast them to the earth.

I step carefully, for everywhere are the bodies of soldiers. Here is the flag, just as it dropped from the color-sergeant's hand. Here an epaulet glitters in crimson and gold; here is a belt of a general, brave in its shining bullion; here, bent and dinted, is the bugle whose silvery voice called into play all the fierce passions, all the ardor of patriotism, all the ambitious hopes that joined in battle and wrought this ruin.

And here, away on the edge of the field, where only the farthest spray from these waves of conflict could reach, my foot had well-nigh fallen upon a child, lying prostrate, half turned on her face. The daintily shod feet peep out of a cloud of silk and lace; the tangled hair of

. . . *The blue-eyed commander comes charging into the parlor in undress uniform—snow-white kilts and zouave cap. "Papa," he inquires, "did oo hear ze battle zis appernoon?"* (Page 137.)

gold, a skein of sunshine, half hides the brow and cheek. There is no sign of life in the beautiful face, and it bears no brand of a cruel blow from the rage of battle. I bend to lift the little figure gently. Deep in the golden hair at the back of the head I see the cleft in the skull. The child; the dainty little girl, whose curls should know no harsher touch than a kiss—the smile still lingering upon the lips—a lovely sacrifice to the hideous Moloch of war.

"Robbie!" I hear the voice of Her Little Serene Highness, "Come dear, gather up your toys. You've left your soldiers scattered over the floor so that papa can scarcely walk across the room without getting into trouble. And somebody has stepped on poor little Bessie's head. I'm afraid she'll have to go to the hospital."

A patter of flying feet, and the blue-eyed commander of both armies, aged six, comes charging into the parlor in undress uniform— snow-white kilts and a zouave cap. He salutes Her Serenity in a military manner of his own, which leaves her somewhat crushed as to ruffle and disordered as to hair. Then, resolving himself into an ambulance corps, he collects the dead and wounded with both hands, scoops them into a box, piles the ordnance on top of them, examines the dead dolly's head for sawdust, and appears to be surprised to discover that it is lined with a big hole.

"Papa," he inquires, "did oo hear ze battle zis appernoon?"

"Yes, Major; I heard the fighting. You appeared to be hotly pressed on both flanks and strongly assaulted in the center."

"We fighted awful," the warrior replied, tossing the artillery into the ambulance on top of a wounded cavalry colonel and the drummer boy, "an' I falled down on my drum and broked my cannon, but grampa can get me annuzzer one. Did my noise bozzer you?"

"No, Major. It helped me."

And the blue eyes of the soldier darted a triumphant laugh into the mother eyes of softest brown, as the Conqueror called his grown-up body-guard together for the evening story and the even song that sounded his nightly "retreat."

138

## XI

"The rich ruleth over the poor, and the borrower is servant unto the lender."—PROVERBS XXII, 7.

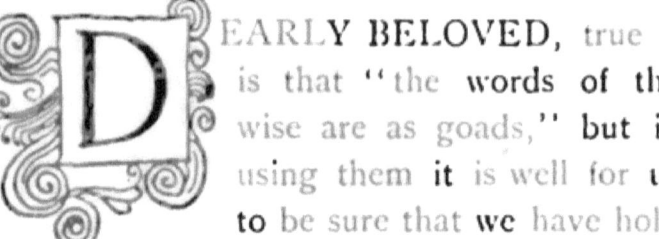

EARLY BELOVED, true it is that "the words of the wise are as goads," but in using them it is well for us to be sure that we have hold of the whip-handle.   Captain Bunsby added a foot-note to human wisdom when he said, "The bearings of this observation lays in the application on it."   True it is that "the rich ruleth over the poor;" that it takes a millionaire to get into the United States Senate, and whoso runneth therefor must open a barrel.   There is a law that comes cheap, and the end thereof is the penitentiary; and there is another law that comes high, and the progress thereof is postponement, and adjournment, and appeal, and temporary stay of proceedings, and chronic stay of judgment, and perpetual stay of execution, and new trials and changes of venue and the end of it never has been reached; but these things are beyond the grasp of a man on a salary.

A cattle king who buyeth 50,000 acres of grazing lands calmly fenceth in 175,000 acres with barbed wire and then grazeth his herds outside the fence, and nobody knoweth the difference, because, say they—

"He owneth all the land from Jericho to Ashdod of the Philistines, and who may say where the Reservation line begins?"

But a poor man who buys a building lot with a fifty-foot front has it measured for him with a Gunther's rule, with a graduated straight-edge and protractor measuring the thousandth part of an inch, and it is graven with a pen of iron on the surveyor's granite corner. And woe is he if his fence fall not within his line. Verily his neighbor, who loveth no man as he loveth his land, will make it warm for him if he encroach by a hair's breadth.

The man about town looketh upon the wine when it is red and costly, and sayeth to the sergeant, "You know me, Johnny," and the sergeant sayeth, "He is good for it," and sendeth him home in a hack. But the rounds-man bringeth in a plebeian who hath a daily job on the dock, and straightway they lock him up and he getteth ten days.

The visiting merchant painteth the town red, and the magistrate before whom he is brought sayeth, "You ought to be ashamed of yourself," and sendeth him home to blush unseen. But his porter cometh to town and assumeth a jag, and the same magistrate sayeth, "You ought to be hanged," and chaineth him upon the stone pile.

Verily wealth is a reassuring, comforting incumbrance. The easiest pew in the synagogue, the front seats at the ball game, the high place on the reviewing stand, are the spoil of the rich. When the rich man lifteth up his head in the hack he scorneth the wheel and its rider.

With only the exception of the messenger boy and the servant-girl, the rich ruleth over the **poor.** **As for her,** she ruleth **the** entire ranch **with a rod of** red **hot iron.** **And for him,** he calleth **no** man "boss," and Time grovels at his feet, asleep. But for the rest **of** us, we are slaves;

"  *  *  *  slaves to a horde
Of petty tyrants, feudal despots; lords
Rich in some dozen paltry villages,
Strong in some hundred spearmen, **only great**
In that strange **spell—a G, n, a, i, g, h, m, e,**—name!"

But, **is it always true that the** "borrower is servant **to the** lender?" **It** was doubtless **so in the** time **of** Solomon, and in a general way it **is** true now, but **a** brighter day has dawned upon the world of borrowers since Solomon owned everything in sight. "The coney are a feeble folk," **but by** building **their** houses **in the rock** they make strong **their** habitation, **and** the walking delegate to-day dictates **terms** to the millionaire that would have cost **him** his head had he whispered them into the crevice of a stone wall **in** the days of Hiram and Solomon.

142

There isn't a man in the world to-day, outside of undiscovered Africa, who can say, "Off with his head," without giving a reason for it, unless he wears a pasteboard crown and carries a scepter which belongs to the property-man. Times change and we change with them. Solomon wrote as a rich lender who had his whole kingdom on a cut-throat mortgage, and thus held the borrower where the hair was short, although the time was long. But all signs fail when you haven't the countersign, and it is a long lane that has no turning. And the lane has turned.

When I was a boy in the halls of my fathers—we had two halls, front and back— in the halls of my fathers, then—I had but one father, it is true, but as he was in no wise a singular man I put him in the plural—in that happy, care-free time, I remember a neighbor who moved out to Illinois shortly after us, and located a claim alongside our own peaceful demesne, where we abode under our own morning-glory vines and fig tree; where children clustered "like olive plants round about the table" three times a day, and fluttered and swarmed like barn swallows all over the place the rest of the time.

The new neighbor came, on the morning of his arrival, to borrow a hatchet. Theirs was nailed up in one of their boxes, he said, and they wanted to unpack their things. That was all right, but I wondered greatly how they packed that hatchet. I had an idea that one of the boys must have got into the last box, and nailed the lid on from the inside. However, I was mistaken; that wasn't the way of it at all. My brother John, to whom I confided my theory, said I might have known better, but I didn't. So we watched the new neighbors unpacking their things all that day, with the most curious interest, every time they opened a new box expecting to see the boy with the hatchet crawl out, a little rumpled and compressed by the long journey from Ohio, but with that certain air of newness that old things long packed are apt to have. I was sorely disappointed when the last box was emptied and no boy seemed to be missed.

The Hadbins—the man's name was O. E.

Hadbin—were neighborly people. Mother said she thought we should like them; but then her gentle nature always thought we should like anybody. Of course, they had no time for cooking the first day, so they ate with us.

That was the western idea in those days. Your house belonged to the new neighbor until he got settled. In that day, if anybody had to go hungry or sleep in the stable, it wasn't the people just off the steamboat or just unloaded from the creaking prairie schooner—for in those days railways were not. It was the old settler who put up with the make-shifts, and he, remembering how he had been welcomed and made comfortable in like manner, never complained, but rather acted as though the new-comer was conferring a favor upon him by accepting his hospitality.

But the next day, after the Hadbins were thoroughly shaken down and settled into place, they sent over and borrowed all the bread we had in the house, and mother, say-

ing that something had evidently gone wrong
with them, sent all the butter we had with it.
I am not sure that the children rejoiced in
this belated opportunity of doing good. As
I chewed dry bread at supper that night, I
ruefully thought of the Hadbins spreading our
good butter upon our soft bread thick as
mortar, and I asked my "blessing" backward. For I hated dry bread. Do yet, although I know it is good for me. I hate
crust, too. Always did. My mother used
to chide me for sneaking my crusts out of
sight without eating them. She said, "Ah,
my boy, I am afraid you will want those good
bread crusts one of these days." I said, so
was I; that was why I didn't eat them at the
time, because if I did, then when I wanted
them they would be gone.

And when any well-meaning guest told me
she thought the crust was the best part of the
bread, I always politely offered to let her have
mine. To this day people are sometimes surprised, when they remove my plate, to see a
little circle of crusts hid around under its edge.

.  .  .  *We saw two of the children coming home from Gregg's with a tub and concluded that the Hadbins were extending their borrowings.*  (Page 147.)

I maintain that bread crust is not edible, that it is not nutritious, that it should no more be eaten by human beings than the rind of an orange. When I see a man eat bread crust willingly, without compulsion, I harbor dark suspicions of him. I believe him to be fit for treasons, stratagems and spoils; a designing and deceitful man.

The next morning one of the children came over to borrow the scythe. It was late in November; there wasn't a thing in all Peoria county to mow, and there never had been any grass on their reservation, anyhow. I suppose now, that they wanted the scythe to cut the bread with; the occasional study of the subject at intervals during all these years has evolved no better solution than that. We gave up the scythe and wondered.

In the afternoon we saw two of the children coming home from Gregg's with a tub, and concluded that the Hadbins were extending their lines to the left, and were reconnoitering all along their immediate front. This surmise was confirmed in the evening, when Mr. Lloyd stopped in for a moment on his way to the store to say that neighbor Hadbin had borrowed all their lamps and he was going down town to get some candles.

"What are candles?"

Oh, well, I don't know that I could tell you just exactly what they were. They "are" not anything. They "were" straight, white things, with a wick that we lit in the evening to see by. "Something like gauze?" Well, yes, dear, something like gauze; something like it; the bill was about ten times stronger than the light.

Well, the Hadbins grew more familiar as you became more intimate with them, and the better acquainted with them you were, the more you knew of them. It is that way with some people. Two or three days after the scythe transaction, Dick Hadbin came and borrowed Charlie's sled. We told him there wouldn't be any snow for nearly a month, but he said he could wait, and went away, patiently dragging the sled through the dust. I began to be a little scared at this indication of communistic spirit, and father said he understood why they borrowed the scythe; it was to have it ready against next summer's haying. But my mother said we mustn't judge them before we knew them better, and went on to say what a sweet voice Mrs. Hadbin had.

"Why, when did you hear it?" one of my sisters asked.

And mother bent her face a little lower over her sewing—I can yet see the faint blush kindling on her cheeks—as she confessed that she heard her asking Mrs. Kent for the loan of her quilting-frame, and "could she tell her where she could borrow some clothes-props and a couple of flat-irons?" The shout of applause that went up saved her from acknowledging that her own department had honored the full requisition for flat-irons and issued half rations of clothes-props.

The Hadbins were Baptists, and I suppose that is one reason why they raided my father's inheritance oftener than they did the borders of Edom and Philistia. They knew the duties and responsibilities of the diaconate. The first Sunday they came to church, Mr.

Hadbin asked my father if he might sit in our pew until they could select one.

"Certainly, Brother Hadbin," and the deacon waved him into it as a prophet might gesture a nation into the promised land. And in filed Brother Hadbin, Sister Hadbin, Ellen Hadbin, George Hadbin, Dick Hadbin, Gad Hadbin, Cynthia Hadbin, and Jane Growl — Hadbin's maid-servant — and the Hadbin twins. They settled in our pew and spread out over the adjoining sections of the court of the Gentiles. We scattered as sheep without a shepherd that Sunday, and afterward camped out on an abandoned claim in the Amen corner that nobody would think of borrowing.

The next day passed quietly and none of our outposts were driven in, but the day after that George and Gad Hadbin came to borrow our dog to go hunting with. We loaned the dog rather sorrowfully, for we were very fond of him. But mother said, "You foolish boys, old Zack will come back himself." That sounded reasonable, but as I am relating a matter of history I can not conscientiously suppress any part of the truth—"Zachary Taylor" never returned. He came home with the Hadbin boys all right—I forgot to mention that they got about a mile out of town before it occurred to them they had forgotten to borrow a gun, and one of them came back and got it—we saw him coming and threw the powder-flask over the fence, and said we hadn't any, so they borrowed powder and shot of Walter Colburn—but never restored himself to us.

Old Zack reported at the fence sometimes, and looked in at us so wistfully that it made our hearts ache; he would stick his head in between the boards to be petted, but he seemed to realize that he had been borrowed, and went back to stay with the rest of our things, until he should be formally returned. Once Mrs. Hadbin came in, and in one of the softest, sweetest, coaxiest voices you ever heard, begged mother to save all the bones for the dog. She said they used theirs for making soap. Not long after that they heard a mouse in their pantry one night and came over next morning to borrow the cat. Now, you know a cat does not belong to a family, but to the house. The cat does not move when the family moves; it stays where it lives. But that cat knew, from the moment Cynthia Hadbin went away with it wrapped up in her apron, that it was a borrowed cat, and it "never came back" to our ranch.

In the silence of the night, once in a while, we could hear Cleopatra—he was really a Mark Antony cat, but my sisters named him Cleopatra when he was little, and he never grew up to his name—singing on the Hadbin wood-shed in plaintive, minor strains, as though his heart was breaking with nostalgia—he was always inclined to nostalgia, and even when he was quite young he would make Rome howl if he was locked out of the kitchen nights—but he returned to the home of his childhood no more. He was borrowed.

In all the world of borrowed things I don't believe any thing can be so completely lost, however, as a borrowed book. Now, if I should drop a book overboard far out at sea;

or if I should let it fall into the crater of Vesuvius, **or if some** sudden tornado should **come** along and blow it off the earth before my astonished eyes, I am not sure that I would be in too great haste to replace it. I think **I would wait, in the** faint hope that may **be, some** how or other, some way or other, some time or other, **it** might **come back** from the realms **of** space; **it** might return from the drifting smoke, the sea might yield **it** up. But when a man comes along and **borrows a** book, then I go down town and buy another copy **for** myself, **if I** want to read it again. **That book is** gone. Isn't it? (Cries of "Yes! Yes!" and "**That's so!**")

So, things ran **on—or** rather, ran off, and **week by week our little** home began to look more desolate **as one** thing **after** another went into the maelstrom, until finally **Mr.** Hadbin, who seldom did **any** borrowing **in** person, struck my father for his autograph on a little thirty-day note for a trifling amount. Father yielded; the note fell due, and the owner of the borrowed name had to pay it himself.

"Don't worry **Mr. Hadbin** about **it**," my

mother pleaded, gently, " he'll pay you some-time."

" That's just when he will," my father replied, grimly. " I haven't said a word to him; he's enough of a business man to know how these things go."

That evening Mr. Hadbin called. He was very angry.

" Deacon," he said, " I understand that you took up that note yourself to-day."

Yes, father said, he did; he didn't want it to go to protest, so he took it up, and Mr. Hadbin could pay him when times were a little easier and—

But Mr. Hadbin waved his hand with a gesture at once injured and sorrowful.

" Well," he said, " I would never have believed it of you. Never. When I heard it, I said it wasn't so—but—." His utterance faltered.

And he was gone. Mad was no name for what he was. He told people he had never been so deceived, never been treated so in all his life. He said he had heard of mean men in Ohio, but he had to come to Illinois to find 'em. And a brother in the church, too.

When he thought of that, he could stand it no longer. He left the Baptist church, after vainly trying to get a rebate on our pew rent for the time he hadn't occupied the pew, and went right off and joined the Children of Light, a new sect that was running a sort of faith-cure fake on commission in a river side cooper-shop.

The week after that, the Hadbins moved. The day they went away they sent us word that they would be beholden to us for nothing, so they sent back all our old things. They sent us, *via* the division fence, three tubs belonging to Gregg, all of Lloyd's lamps, except the parlor camphene lamp, which had exploded when they set it on the kitchen stove, Knowlton's wheel-barrow, Weston's buggy harness, Mrs. Phillips's preserving kettle, John Shepherd's plow, Mrs. Tapping's quilting-frames, and a great variety of things belonging to everybody in the neighborhood except ourselves. We announced a " reception," the neighbors came in, identified their property and took it away, and we saw our own things and the Hadbins no more.

Since then, often I have thought that when Poor Richard wrote " He that goes a borrowing goes a sorrowing," he must have meant that one fellow went a borrowing and the other fellow went a sorrowing.

# THE KATYDID IN OPERA

## XII

OUR country opera is like Vog-
ner's music. The untutored
mind can not appreciate its
beauties, its masterly use of
the recitative, the strong sim-
plicity of its "leitmotif," enriched by laby-
rinthine combinations and the beautiful
accessories of the orchestra, each player a
composer, a soloist and a specialist.

Last night the orchestra was unusually
strong; tree-toad and cricket, droning beetle,
two whip-po'-wills, a solitary owl; two or
three baying dogs just far enough away, a
sheep bell that tinkled softly at broken intervals; now and then a sleepy twitter from the
apple tree where the robins live, as though

the birds could keep awake just long enough
to sing one or two slumbrous bars, falling
asleep in the middle of a half-note; the frogs,
with their great double basses, down in the
sedgy pond; once a chanticleer fugue, that
drifted over the stage from east to west, as
Dominique and Leghorn caught their cue;
and all the time the wind, whispering through
the hedges and giving the best imitation of
the rustling of maple leaves at night that you
never heard equaled by ventriloquist or vio-
lins on a lime-lighted stage.

That is one specialty in which the orchestra on our farm excels—the imitation of
sounds from the forest. But as I said, you
have to be educated up to it. My friend
Streaton Alleigh spent a few days with me
last week, and one afternoon we were listening to a cat-bird giving an imitation of the
thrush.

"Say," said Alleigh, "you ought to keep
a gun here on the piazza and blow that thing
out of the tree when he comes shrieking
around that way. That's enough to give a
graven image the headache."

. . . *He took me to a concert, and a whistling woman came out and said: "I will now give you an imitation of a cat-bird."* (Page 150.)

The next day I went to the city with him. He took me to a concert, and a whistling woman came out and said:

" I will now give you an imitation of the song of the cat-bird."

Streaton Alleigh clapped his hands until he split his gloves.

" Say! old man," he cried after the second encore, "wasn't that great? Did you ever hear anything like that?"

And when I said I thought I had, he said he guessed I hadn't. "Not out in Bryn Mawr you haven't," he said warmly; "you haven't got money enough in your whole township to get that woman to go out there and whistle for you."

Nevertheless, I have never heard an imitation of the robin equal to the one given by another robin. The trouble with most people is that they don't stay out here long enough to learn the language. Now it may be that you can enjoy German opera without knowing "nein" from "ja."

I once attended Italian opera, in which everybody sang English except the tenor and

**soprano,** and I understood them better than **I did** any of the others, although I don't know enough Italian to drive away an organ-grinder. But to enjoy the opera on the farm you must understand the words. No librettos are printed, but you listen to the music **for a** few years, and then begin your interpretation. And of half-a-dozen people who listen in silence, on the same evening, no two will hear the same **opera.** If there is somebody blab, blab, blabbing **all the** time, of course you can't understand **a** word.

In the season, **we have** music every night. The silence of **a** summer night in the country is a silence to which you can listen; "soft stillness and the night become the touches of sweet harmony." Come out and live in this musical silence for awhile if you "want to hear the old band play"; listen to it, night after night, until you **have** learned to love this melodious stillness, and **then** if you wish, go back to brick walls and paved streets, and lie down **to be** lulled to sleep by the varied pleasing **of** rattling hacks, crashing trucks, thundering fire engines and jingling trolley bells.

It is pleasant, as we attend the opera night after night, to note the advent of the old favorites. Our artists teach their children to sing and play so exactly like themselves that we scarcely realize we have a new cast every season. We think of it and speak of it, perhaps, in the closing days of the summer. The music, I grant you, is somewhat melancholy in the autumn time. There will come some sharp, keen night when the orchestra is very meager. Only a few hardy little musicians appear. And they do not play very long; they cut the opera in every scene, and play only long enough, probably, to save the box receipts, then they pack up their instruments and hurry away to the warmest corners of stack yard and stubble field. We observe on these nights that the voices of the soloists display no hoarseness, however. So long as they do sing, they sing their best.

But in spite of that, the autumnal performance on the whole is pathetic. For they choose mournful themes; they sing of the golden summer that is gone, and their music shudders with the dread of frosty nights and the cruel winter that is coming; they play dirges for their dead comrades; they sing of purple aster and royal golden-rod; the plumy lances of the iron weed in old meadows; the yellow primrose, gleaming like stars in the gray twilight; the ghostly thistle-down, drifting over the reedy marshes where the fire-flies died; of grotesque shadows in the old stump lot; of cold winds, creeping with eerie whispers across the fields where the corn stands in ragged shocks with stiffened blades; of wheeling colonies of summer birds that flecked the fields with restless shadows as they gathered the clans together and sped away to the gayety of the winter resorts; of faded ferns in the glens, of withered grasses in the fence corners and blighted flowers in the old-fashioned gardens, until at last the merry voices cease, all the daughters of music are brought low, the last little soloist sings his good-bye song with a brave little trill in his far-reaching voice, and goeth the way of all grasshoppers.

Nevertheless, happier he who lives to sing

the faded glories and the joys of the summer gone, than his ill-fated comrade, who, with many a song unsung, was "yanked" off the sweet-potato vine, when July days were bright and high, by relentless fate, with a fan-tail and big red wattles. Brave and eventful and joyous have been the days of his life; for the years of the grasshopper being but as a summer that is told resembles much our own. He plays, he sings, he suffers, he dies; his life is full — er hat geliebt und gelebet. From the boy in the farm-house to the trout in the brook and the fowl in the barn-yard, he has enemies and enemies, and like god-like man, ofttimes he saves his life by using his good swift legs.

But last night, just in the midst of the overture—it was a spirited passage descriptive of the earthquake—the tree-frogs, with their piccolos, were showing how the ground trembled, and the cricket was imitating a shrieking woman who was afraid to stay in the house and didn't dare come out—just as the orchestra made the "rest" to indicate the interval between the shocks, the katydid (stage name; family name *Cyrtophyllum concavum*), made his appearance. He wore a green suit, same as last year, with long over-wing covers, of cut-away shape, and as he struck the first notes on his taborets, the whole house cried,

"There's the katydid!".

He did not sing very long; he never does, on a first night, but his presence added strength to the opera. The ever popular barytone was here and everybody was glad to hear him again.

"She" does not sing. Katy, herself, is voiceless. A dutiful, quiet, homekeeping little Katy, hiding away with her master all day among the leaves, when he is quiet as herself. For he is a true foot-light artist; he will not sing until the stars are lighted. And then, when nightly he ascends to the higher branches of the trees and proclaims to the world that "Katy did," the mother of his little katies is silent with womanly wisdom.

Never a word does she speak, not a note does she sing in reply, though all night

long he should declare that "she did." If
ever she should lose her patience and reply to
his accusing song, what thrilling domestic
revelations might we not expect? In crimi-
nation and recrimination, in bill and cross-
bill, rejoinder and sur-rejoinder, plea and
replication, it would all come out. But, calm
and serene in her conscious innocence, she
answers not a word. Sometimes, in a fit of
masculine irritation at having his own way
unopposed, he flatly contradicts himself and
sings "Katy didn't; she didn't; she didn't;"
man-like, choosing to take issue with himself rather than have no one with whom to
quarrel.

Really, after listening to him for many
years, I have no idea that she ever did anything so very dreadful. They have never
separated; they live happily together; and
I think it is only some good-natured threat of
his to tell some joke which he holds over her
head. But whatever it was, he never tells it,
and I think it happened so long ago that he
has forgotten it, and sings his song just as most
people sing a hymn, without the slightest

idea what it means. Maybe he doesn't sing
the words of the original song, anyhow; there
may be hymn tinkers among the katydids, as
there are among "humans," and, in that
case, investigation and research will never
discover the original language of his song.
But whatever it is, she never contradicts him;
she never sings with him, even in good-natured duet. For it is a cold, unfeeling scal-
pel to thrust into the spinal column of miles
of good poetry and sentiment, but the icy,
steel-blue fact is that my lady Katydid is
voiceless. But then, he would not sing,
either, were she not there to listen. She may
not voice the song; she does a great deal
better; she inspires the singer, and thus she
creates the song.

So he sings for us in the lengthening nights.
And as he sings, some there are in his audi-
ence who hear, as in a dream, the songs he
sung on yester-eve; songs of that happy Past,
"whose yesterdays look backward with a
smile." To them his strident solo is a talis-
man that opens wide the doors to Memory-
land, with the old walks we only take when

time is swifter than a thought **and** longer than eternity.

**Down** winding paths beneath **the** whispering oaks; through tangled grasses in the orchard glooms; across the foot-bridge where the brook goes singing softly all night long; through forest vistas, where the sunset **loiters with its** benediction **to** the ·day—all **the** dear **paths** that **only lovers know and** love; even **by shadowed** ways that **lead** through **valleys** where the damps are chill; through desert paths **of** tears, and rankling pain, where Marah's waters darken in the solemn pools; and all the way and all the **time the** clasp **of a** fluttering hand, the gleam **of** starlight in the love-lit **eyes.** Until, at last, **the song and** the dream lead on to where the singing brook, **its** laughter **silenced and its** music hushed, **deepens** into **the** darkly flowing river, and in the morning light that lights our sun, the shadows pass away forever.

**Ah,** katydid, in other worlds than ours you must have sung and learned new melodies **since** all the days were gold and all the world was young. For who, in this bright world of ours, this iand of hope and song, this sunlit world of happy hearts and summer skies, could teach your tiny harp these minor chords? Where could you learn, on all this laughing earth, that Joy and Sorrow, sisters born of Love, walk ever hand in hand? Where could you learn to sing of tears and loneliness?

# THE OLD ROAD SHOW

## XIII

ADIES and gentlemen, one and all, great and small, rich and poor alike, bear in mind and remember that this is the first and last, the best and the only opportunity this living generation will ever have to look upon these wonderful curiosities of nature and art, gathered and garnered from every part and corner of the inhabitable globe and the undiscovered islands of the sea. Bear in mind, too, that each and every performance, prodigy, freak, and phenomenon represented and described in the bills is in a like and exact manner performed and exhibited within the canvas—the large lady, the wild man of Borneo,

the bearded **woman, the great** snake and **the live** lion—and a quatovadollah takes you in to **see** them **all!**

**Have your** change ready, please, as you **ask** for tickets, and remember that **if** the show and performance does not give **you** full **and** entire satisfaction **as** guaranteed, your money will **be** refunded at the ticket-wagon.

**Here you are, ladies** and **gentlemen, the only** genuine **five-toed Wizard of Finance ever exhibited outside a** cage, **born** in Amer-**ica, but captured in** Canada with the bonds **in his possession,** striped around the **body and both** legs with horizontal bars, **and** his hair cut close to the other end like—if **you** creep under that canvas, my son, you will get yourself brained with a tent-pin—and his cage surrounded by shorn lambs **the** same as it is saw in **his** native jungle.

**Yes, sir!** And here **you have** the **great American** bird show, passing strange **and** beggaring description—the latest Flyer from the Stock Exchange, and the wonderful Pair **o' dice bird,** which wears his bones in his tal-

. . . "*The large lady, the wild man of Borneo, the bearded woman, the great snake, and the live lion—and a quatoradollah takes you in to see them all!*" (Page 170.)

ents and devours strangers from the country; a flock of lame Ducks from Wall street, and the great American Tariff Bill, the only bird in the living world which has no wings, is born without feet, has no gizzard, and twelve pairs of lungs, with which it utters its mournful note thirteen months in the year so piercing loud that it can be heard from sea to sea on a still night, and wherever it is heard it drives men mad!

And the crow, the great black Bitter River Crow, *Americanus hadtotakus*—carry that dollar bill back to the man who made it, my friend, and tell him he'll have to do better than that or he cawn't never pass it on this show—which is a favorite article of diet with many eminent statesmen, the vast proportion of brimstone contained in solution with gall rendering it a most invaluable tonic and brain food, and you can pass into the tent and see it for a quatovadollah!

Bear in mind and remember! In no other country on the face of this globe can you behold this collossal aggregation of marvelous spectacles! The White Elephant of America! A Colossal Colossus! the biggest beast that breathes! Bearing on his stupendious back the Venezuelean boundary, the Cuban revolution, the Eastern question, the New Woman, the Flying Machine, and the Dress Reform, and nobody knows how to train him nor how to get off his load! A half interest in the show is offered to any man who can lead him safely once around the ring.

Walk in and see the City Robin, who builds his nest in the state capitol, the council chamber and other safe places, lines it with other birds' notes, and holds on to the combination with both claws while he broods his young with the other. When he raises his note a little pitch higher it is a sign of spring, and it's a spring that lands him in Canada where he becomes a *rara avis*, wakes with the due in the morning and sleeps with the missed at night; a cuir colored bird until he begins to Sing Sing, when he turns gray, puts on stripes and moults his plumage, retaining only the feathers which line his nest outside his cage; a most wonderful bird indeed, hard to catch, harder to keep, and hardest of all **to** let alone.

**He** has five claws **on** each foot, and would have more **if** he thought there was anything more for him **to** grab—keep that hand-organ a-goin', young fellow; don't go to sleep with five thousand people standing around here dyin' **for** music! **And** one little quarter **of a** dollah **takes you into each and every canvas!** Only a quatovadollah **to go in and see** the City Robin—no, sir, you didn't carry no water for the Elephant—which, being light-fingered, can work in the dark, and **it** costs more to catch him than he is **worth** when he is caught, **for** you can't sell **him,** and while everybody wants **to** catch him, nobody wants **to** keep him, **and you** can see him inside **the** big **tent for a** quatovadollah, and cheap at **half** the money.

A quatovadollah! Remember, this **exhibition** positively closes with the **final** performance, and will not appear here again until its return. Pause at the first cage on the right **as** you go in and view the justly celebrated American Pelican, the *Liarius awful-*

173

*ius* of Linnæus, with scales on its legs where-
with it gets a weigh with the fish it does **not**
catch, and which comprise its food—that is
correct, sir, **three** tickets, pass right in, yourself, wife and daughter, and **the little boy**
hiding behind his mother's skirts will have **to**
wait **outside** with me until you **come** back,
unless you can raise another quarter, **sir**; yes
sir, **we** have to have eyes in our fingers, the
back of **our** necks, the tips of **our** toes and **the**
heels of **our** boots **if we** want **to** get four quarters of money **out of** a dollar's **worth of pa-
trons,** sir.

The great American Pelican is **fond of**
his **early** bitterns **and** takes a swallow **before**
he goes to fish, **and if** one doesn't satisfy
him toucan, and he can get it right **in the**
bird show; he's a hard bird to gull, **for he**
carries a pocket pistol when he goes a-fishing,
and knows how to cockatoo; nothing **pleases
him** so much as a gosling, because **a soft an-**
ser turneth away wrath. He carries his **bait**
in a jug, and his trout **rod in a** pipe case; **he**
can fish all day and **never** be within five miles
**of water,** because he fishes **with his mouth,**

and you can pass right in and see him fish and hear him lie for a quatovadollar.

And still they come and still they crowd! For a thousand years may pass and the sun will never shimmer and shine upon a show like this. Keep to the right as you go in and pass rapidly in front of the cages. Buy your tickets now and you will have plenty of time to show the children the wild animals before the performance begins in the circus tent proper.

Pause a moment before the cage with a glass front and contemplate the American Dodo, captured with incredible toil and at limitless expense in the wilds of Nooyawk-enwhy. This remarkable bird is found in its imperfect state nowhere else in the world; it is hatched in an unfurnished nest on the tenth floor back, one at a time, with one glass eye and no brains, half fledged at birth and never grows another pin feather; takes its nutriment from the head of a cane by suction, and is never weaned, tamed or brained; sleeps under the bed instead of on it; remains out of doors during the rain; has no salary and

175

but one note, which it utters at intervals, saying "Haw—aw," in a melancholy inflection,
which drives the ordinary loon of the lakes to
idiocy with imbecile envy.

The Dodo is a nestling fowl until its twen-
tieth year, when it partially sheds its down
and puts on an ass's skin, which fits it like
the paper on the wall, and in which it eats,
sleeps, and would eventually die if it had suffi-
cient energy to do anything so useful. Great
care is taken to preserve it, there being deep-
rooted fear among naturalists that if any
means of killing this bird should be discovered it would soon become extinct.
When you see it, give it a cigarit and hear
it say "haw—aw." It has been known to
utter that sound thrice within a single hour,
but the effort is very exhausting. This singular bird is a hybrid, and is supposed to
be a cross between a gosling and a squab,
inheriting the brains of the one and the
softness of the other. Do not poke at it
with your parasol, lady, it angers it, and
when violently enraged it becomes uncontroll-

able **and** fades, and you can buy **a matinee** ticket and see it for a quatovadollah.

Roll up, tumble **up!** Bear in mind **that** the three great allied shows in one admit you **to** each **and** every exhibition under every canvas for the pitiful sum of one quatovadollah, including a chaste and refined presentation of high caste Afro-American minstrelsy at **the** conclusion of the performance **in** the ring.

Pass around to the upholstered sty, and gaze upon the Man-faced Bristled Hog. This disgusting beast is born ugly and roots naturally; occupies four seats in the railway car, smokes in the ladies' cabin, takes three chairs **on** the steamer deck, one **for its** hams, one **for** its hoofs, and one **for** its wraps; it will **lie** and fight for the last lower berth in **a** sleeper; spits **on** the sidewalk; when awake **it** grunts, when asleep **it** snores; when eating it sucks and smacks. It dreads solitude and is never found alone, always seeking the crowds in the city and at summer hotels. It crackles peanuts and munches caramels at the theater, talks aloud at **the** opera, and grunts the tunes **at** the concert. **It** is long-lived, and can only

12                    177

be killed **by** shaving its bristles and **compel-**
ling **it to be** decent for half-an-hour. **It is**
only useful, after death, as **a** fertilizer, the
vilest cannibals refusing to partake of its flesh
**after** having seen the living Hog.

**And** another **goes in** for a quatovadollah!
**Four** more pass **in!** Yourself, your **wife,**
your son and your daughter—another **home**
made happy, another heart made glad, **and**
another ticket sold **for** the great allied show,
kindergarten and school **of** equestration **and**
natural history, eulogized by bench, bar and
bishop, **endorsed by** the clergy, patronized
**by** the crowned heads **of** Europe, **and** visited
**by** countless thousands of the people! The
great moral mastodon of all great **moral mas-**
todons ever collected into one gigantic, **col-**
lossal and measureless agglomeration **of** prod-
igy, wonder and miracle under **one** cluster of
canvas canopies!

Here **you** behold **the** omniverous **Ameri-**
can Office Hunter, the howling wolf **of the**
wilderness, littered **in a** Coke oven, lines
his **den** with Blackstones, and burrows **in**
the Cayote-house. Hunts in pairs and never

divides with the other wolf; eats all the
time, never gets enough, is always hungry, ravenous and lien. The more he
gets the more he expects, the louder he
howls and the hungrier he is; he has a bill
like a snipe, a tale like a comet, more clause
than a tarantula, and more turns than a cork-
screw. He has a bill like a duck to show
that he's a quack, claws like a mole, because
his ways are dark, and they're webbed like a
loon's, for he's quick to take water, dives
deep and holds his breath for an hour at a
time. This animal is born in office, and soon
dies when removed from his native element;
he is a labor reformer from the tip of his nose
to the corners of his eyes, and a bald monop-
olist from the eyebrows to the tip of his ears;
one ear is protection and the other is free
trade; and his neck is anything to beat either
of them. Democrat down the left leg and
Republican up the right; one foot is Saddu-
cee and the other is Pharisee; and he believes
in Tom Paine and the Apostles' creed.
Whichever way you stroke his fur it lies
smooth as silk, for if there is one thing the

American Politician **is** consistent in it is smooth lying.

Have your change ready as soon as you **come up to the ticket** wagon, please, **and** look out as you go in **for the** jail bird **in** the brass cage near the **door,** he's very wary. How wary, sir? Cassowary, **to** be sure, Mr. Smartweed, and that entitles you to a free pass outside the canvas where you can look at the pictures for nothing while this gentleman goes inside and stays all afternoon **for a** quatovadollah.

**Pass in** rapidly **now,** and gather around the ring **side and see the** Wild Ass of the Desert **led in to browse** on **the** nutritious cactus of his native wilds! Already he has bet a wheelbarrow ride and a potato race on the **next** election; he will go around the ring **and** take up presidential votes **to** show how little sense he **ever** had. He whistles **aloud in the railway** car and learns to read with the newspaper of the **hotel;** he wears **a** liver-pad and **an electric** belt; believes **in the** blue glass cure for everything; indorses **a** patent medicine **to get** his picture in the papers; touches a buzz saw to see if it is going, and gets his hair cut Saturday night. He thinks there is tobacco in cigarettes, believes that Moses wrote the Gospel according to Luke, and the other Isaiah wrote the Pentateuch; doesn't believe the fish swallowed Jonah, but will swallow any thing himself that you offer him, provided it is sufficiently unreasonable; rejects the first chapter of Genesis, but accepts Robinson Crusoe, and believes that he is eating bread and butter when the waiter knows that he gave him alum and oleo. Stand back a little and see him prance around the ring; it doesn't take much to start him and nothing can stop him. Lift the flap of the tent a little and you may see him snuff up the east wind on which he feeds.

Bear in mind and remember, then! Every day in the week, and every week in the year, this unrivaled alliance of colossal equescurricular entertainments and museum of natural and living curiosities will give three·exhibitions daily and one each evening with an entire change of programme at each and every entertainment. Remember that we are daily

181

adding to a collection **already** surpassing anything **in** the known world, presenting **to** your **view** a spectacle that kings **and em-perors have** longed **to see, and died without** seeing.

**The** lady **with** three sets **of teeth, one in** her mouth and two **on** her dressing-table; the only Living Statesman who has gone out of politics without being kicked **out;** the only living deaf **and** dumb pugilist; a private night-watchman standing wide awake on **duty;** a **church choir** singing praise to the **Prince of Peace without a row;** an imported **actress with but one** husband—**her** own and only.

Also, will arrive **on** next steamer, **con-**signed **to** this show: **A** mouse, chased by a woman; a walking delegate at work; **a** fat poet; an industrious labor reformer; **a** government clerk refusing **an** increase of salary; a minister getting **one;** and these **and a** thousand other wonders **to be** seen nowhere else in all the wide creation, **and** all **for the little** sum **of a** quatovadollah!

# THE VACATION OF MUSTAPHA

## XIV

AM, by choice, a dweller in the country. You have guessed as much by the freckles on my grammar and the sunburn on my rhetoric. I love people I admire the madding crowd, but at a distance. When I go to town, it is high holiday with me. I walk the unyielding pavements sideways, staring in at the shop windows. I read the signs, and find in them much palatable intellectual pabulum. I carry my bundles under my arms, not knowing that they may be sent to the station for me. I stand with the giddy throng that hangs spellbound on the eloquence of the fakir selling patent glue or magic knife sharpeners, or an

183

all-round tool which **will** shave, curl hair, **cut** glass, **draw** nails, stretch carpets, **saw scroll** work, open cans, and solder. **To go to** town **on** the **fourth of** July **is** worth the waiting through **a** long winter. But **to go to** town **on** circus day is not a joy. **It is an** ecstasy.

**And yet,** always **am I** glad **to** shake **off** the dust **of** the city and get back **to** the coun-**try** with its peace and quiet. After I have **been shoved about** and elbowed and jostled **by people who are either busy** or **crazy, I never can** tell which; **after I have** been as-saulted **by** vigorous women ballasted with **market** baskets loaded, apparently, with stones and other hard articles; after **I** have **been** scattered by other women with sharp elbows like Scythian chariots; run down by wild-eyed **men** chasing after trolley cars; butted into the street **or** the show window by **other frantic men** rushing **for** trains, and run **over** by yelping bicyclers, and after **I** myself have run over, **or** rather crawled over, a few fleet-footed messenger **boys,** glad **am I** to limp to the station, and hunt for my lost railway ticket all the way back to the lanes, and fields and quiet woods.

Oh, I have no set antipathy to the city. I think that town is a good place to go to. The country is only a place to live. I know there are some good people who live in town. Town is, no doubt, the best place for some people. So is jail. I have the same compassionate feeling for people in the city that I have for people in jail, because I have so often observed how glad they are to get out of it. But people who see the country only in the summer time lose its most beautiful aspects. The country is not very lovely in midsummer. That is the period of its greatest discomfort; its most depressing monotony.

I love the stillness of the country sunset, when peace broods over the earth with cloud-tinted wings. I love to watch the daylight fade into twilight, and evening deepen into dusky night; to watch the stars come out over the plumy trees and march in resplendent battalions across the silent fields of the skies. I would love to see the rosy

185

fingered hours draw aside the curtains of the
dawn, and hail Aurora as she comes dancing
through the portals of the morning, if I had
time. But at that early hour I am too busy,
thinking how comfortable I am, to get up.
It is much better, I think, to meet Aurora
with a face as smiling as her own, at the
breakfast table.

There is an atmosphere of " silken rest "
in the country that is ever delightful to the
care-worn children of the town, like " sleep
after toyle, port after stormie seas." Most
vividly do I remember, as we are all prone to
remember most vividly those things which
never happened—some of us, perhaps, being
a little more prone than others—a man who
once upon a time, flying " out of the dust of
the town of the king," sought repose and
recuperation in the " odors of ploughed field
or flowery mead." Now, it happened of
this man, whose name was Mustapha—Mustapha Rest—that he had called unto him his
physician and said:

" Lo, I am wearied with much work; care
and worry have done me up; the hand of

exhaustion is upon me, and I am even now at death's door. I am not afraid to die, but I don't want to."

And it was so that his physician looked at his tongue, felt his pulse and cried,

" Twodollahs!" (for this was an oath by which all physicians in the reign of the good Caliph swore). " Of a verity thou must have repose! Flee unto the Valley of Rest, close thine eyes in dreamy nothingness; hold back thy hands from toil and thy brain from care, or thou wilt be laid by the heels and that without remedy. Bismillah! Three-dollahs!"

And when Mustapha heard him he arose, and put his business into the hands of his confidential clerk, who had already put his hands on the most of it, and was even now getting ready to skip with the rest of it. And Mustapha went away to the Valley of Rest, there to abide with his Uncle Ben, whom he had not seen for lo, so many years. Now his Uncle Ben was an husbandman. He dwelt in the Valley of Rest; the mountains of repose were roundabout him, and the plains of

comfort were the meadows of his tillage
But his post-office was Getthere-Eli. And
he was rich and well-favored; strong as an
ox, and healthy as plantain weed. Ofttimes
he rose up and boasted with a loud voice that
there was not a lazy bone in his body. And
in every bed-room in his house there was
hung up a chromo-text in many colors and
loud letters—'' The Lord Hates a Sluggard.''

But Mustapha wist not that it was so.

Now, when he reached his Uncle Ben's
they received him with great joy, and came
forth to meet him, and shouted at him and
cried out his name with an exceeding loud
shout, albeit they were close beside him, and
made him so nervous that he forgot his own
name. And they saluted him, saying,
'' Howdicuznmusti?'' which is to say, '' How
do you do, Cousin Mustapha?'' And he
answered them and said, '' Horry Yunk'
Ben?'' which by interpretation is, '' How are
you, Uncle Benjamin?''

And when even was come they sat down
to supper. And they placed before him a
supper of homely viands, well cooked, and

piled up on his plate like the wreck of a
freight car. And when he could not eat all,
and ask for more, they laughed him to scorn.

And after supper, they sat up with him
and talked with him concerning relatives of
whom he knew naught, and of whom he had
never before so much as heard. And he
spake at random, and lied unto them, for he
had been a politician in his youth and gov-
erned not his tongue. Moreover, he was
ashamed because of his ignorance. Wherefore he told them that he had a letter from
Uncle Issachar last week, and he was well and
liked the country.

Now, they all knew that Uncle Issachar
had been shot in another man's sheep pen,
out in Colorado, three years ago, when the
moon was in the dark. But Mustapha wist
not that it was so. And he said that Uncle
Ezra died in California last winter. But Uncle Ezra was alive, and was even then in the
house of Uncle Ben, bed-ridden and stricken
in years. But Mustapha knew it not, for he
was dead for sleep, and talked only to keep
himself awake.

And when they had all the fun they wanted on family affairs, they talked politics. Now, Mustapha had been an old-line Whig and an Abolitionist, when such things were, and he was now a Republican of the deepest dye, such as would get up in the night at any time to kill a Mugwump. But Uncle Ben was a hickory Democrat, and had owned slaves before the war, when he lived in Maryland, and he was postmaster at the town of Getthere-Eli until such time as he was fired out.

And they spent a very pleasant evening.

And about one o'clock of the morning they went to bed.

And it was so that four boys slept with Mustapha, for the bed was wide. And they slumbered crosswise in the bed, and kicked Mustapha black and blue all the night, insomuch that he closed not his eyes in slumber, neither slope he a wink. And it was so.

And at the fourth hour after midnight, his Uncle Ben smote upon his back, and cried unto him, saying:

"Awake! Arise! Rustle out of this and wash your face, for the liver and bacon is

. . . And when they had all the fun they wanted on my family affairs, they talked politics. (Page 190.)

fried and breakfast is ready. You will find
the soap and towel on the bench by the
smoke-house door, and the trough is down
by the horse well at the end of the cow lot.''

And when they had eaten, Uncle Ben spake
unto him and said, '' Come, let us take a
stroll around the farm.''

And they walked that morning as it were
the space of eleven miles. And Mustapha
wore tight boots, such as are made in town.

And it was their hap to light upon some
men-servants at work in the hay-field. And
they set Mustapha upon an exceeding high
and toppley wagon, and his Uncle Ben taught
him how to build a load of hay. Then they
drove to the barn, where he taught him how
to unload it. Then they girded up their
loins and walked four miles into the forest,
and Uncle Ben taught him how to chop wood.
And his hands were soft, and they blistered
like new paint in August.

And the morning and the evening were the
first day, and Mustapha wished that he were
dead.

And after supper his Uncle Ben said:

" Come, let us go out and have some fun."
And they hooked up a team and drove nine
miles over in Timber township, where the boys
had a dance. And they danced until the
second hour in the morning.

And when the next day was come—which
was not long, for the night was spent when
they got home—Uncle Ben took him out in
the blazing sun and taught him how to build
a rail-fence. And when even was come
Mustapha was so full of slivers that the hedge-
hog, seeing him, cried, " Behold my brother !"
And the porcupine called after him and said,
" Thou art my father and mother, and sister
and brother, and all my relatives by mar-
riage !"

And it was so.

And that night there was a wedding over
in Hooshaw, and they all went, and made
merry, and ate slabs of cake nine inches thick
and weighing thirty-two ounces to the half
pound.

Nevertheless, when they went to bed at
three o'clock in the morning, Mustapha was
asleep when he got out of the wagon. And

he walked up stairs with his eyes shut. And he undressed not, but lay down to sleep across the four boys with his boots on.

But the four lads wept, and besought him that he would get up, and he might sleep on the outside. Whereupon he answered them roughly, and smote the nearest one, and prayed that he himself might die before breakfast time.

But breakfast had an early start and got there first.

After breakfast his Uncle Ben took him down to the creek and taught him how to shear sheep. And when even was come, they hooked up after supper and drove to spelling-school, out in district number three. And they got home the first watch after midnight, and Uncle Ben marveled that it was yet so early. And he lighted a cob pipe and sat up and told Mustapha all about the forty acres he bought of Moses Stringer last fall to join on his south eighty, so as to finish out that half.

And when Mustapha went to bed that night he bethought him of a dose of strychnine he had in his trunk. So he said his prayers twice, and took it.

But the youngest boy was restless that night and kicked all the poison out of Mustapha's system in ten minutes.

And the next morning, while it was yet night, Uncle Ben took him out into a field that was nigh unto the house, and taught him how to dig potatoes. And the sun was hot. And it was so that when he bent over the blood rushed to his head and set his eyes on fire, and when he rose up his back brake.

And after supper was eaten, Uncle Ben remembered that there was a revival at Bethesda church. So they hitched up the bay colt and went.

Now, there were present three preachers beside the pastor, an evangelist and a theological student and one lay preacher. And they all improved the time. And when they got home, about midnight, they sat up and talked about the meeting until bed time.

Now, when Mustapha was home, it was his rule to go to bed the third hour after his dinner, and he arose not the next **day** until **the** sun was high.

So the day **after the** meeting, when **his Uncle Ben** would take him out to the boundary of his farm and show him how to build an exceeding long line-fence of post-and-rail, Mustapha beguiled him into the forest, **saying, " Lo,** here **is** the boss **tree for a gate-** post.''

**And when his** Uncle Ben came **to look at** it Mustapha smote him thrice **across** the **neck** with a dog-wood maul and fled, and gat **himself** home.

**And** Mustapha sent for his physician and called **him** names. And **he** said he was tired **to** death; and he turned his **face** to the wall and **died.** So Mustapha sojourned no longer in the Valley **of** Rest, **for he** was **gathered to** his fathers.

But **his** Uncle **Ben, who** came **to** the funeral, and had to do all his weeping with one eye, because that Mustapha had knocked **out** the other **one,** said that Mustapha was **too** lazy to breathe, and **he had no** get-up-and-get **about** him.

195

But Mustapha wist not what they said, for he was dead. And they divided up his property amongst themselves, and made merry.

And they bought no tombstone for him, for they said they had no time, and if he wanted one he should have attended to it himself while he was yet alive.

And it was so.

# THE BRAKEMAN AT CHURCH

## XV

NE bright winter morning, the twenty-ninth day of December, Anno Domini 1879, I was journeying from Lebanon, Indiana, where I had sojourned Sunday, to Indianapolis. I did not see the famous cedars, and I supposed they had been used up for lead-pencils, and moth-proof chests, and relics, and souvenirs; for Lebanon is right in the heart of the holy land. That part of Indiana was settled by Second Adventists, and they have sprinkled goodly names all over their heritage. As the train clattered along, stopping at every station to trade off some people who were tired of traveling for some other people who were tired of staying at home, I got out my writing-pad,

pointed a pencil, and wondered what manner of breakfast I would be able to serve for the ever hungry " Hawkeye " next morning.

I was beginning to think I would have to disguise some " left-overs " under a new name, as the thrifty house-keeper knows how to do, when my colleague, my faithful yoke-fellow, who has many a time found for me a spring of water in the desert place—the Brakeman, came down the aisle of the car. He glanced at the tablet and pencil as I would look at his lantern, put my right hand into a cordial compress that abode with my fingers for ten minutes after he went away, and seating himself easily on the arm of the seat, put the semaphore all right for me by saying:

" Say, I went to church yesterday."

" Good boy," I said, " and what church did you attend? "

" Guess," was his reply.

" Some Union Mission chapel?" I ventured.

" N—no," he said, " I don't care to run on these branch roads very much. I don't get a chance to go to church every Sunday,

THE BRAKEMAN AT CHURCH

and when I can go, I like to run on the main
line, where your trip is regular, and you
make schedule time, and don't have to wait
on connections. I don't care to run on a
branch. Good enough, I reckon, but I don't
like it."

"Episcopal?" I guessed.

"Limited express!" he said, "all parlor
cars, vestibuled, and two dollars extra for a
seat; fast time, and only stop at the big sta-
tions. Elegant line, but too rich for a brakeman. All the trainmen in uniform; conductor's punch and lanterns silver-plated;
train-boys fenced up by themselves and not
allowed to offer anything but music. Passengers talk back at the conductor. Trips
scheduled through the whole year, so when
you get aboard you know just where you're
going and how long it will take you. Most
systematic road in the country and has a
mighty nice class of travel. Never hear of a
receiver appointed on that line. But I didn't
ride in the parlor car yesterday."

"Universalist?" I suggested.

"Broad gauge," the Brakeman chuckled;

199

" does too **much** complimentary business to be prosperous. Everybody travels on a pass. Conductor doesn't **get a** cash fare once **in** fifty miles. Stops **at** all way-stations and **won't run into** anything but a union depot. No smoking-car allowed on the train because **the** company doesn't own enough brimstone to head **a** match. Train orders are rather vague, though; and I've noticed the trainmen don't 'get along very well with the passengers. **No,** I didn't go **on the broad** gauge, though **I have** some good friends on that road who are the **best** people in the world. **Been** running **on it** all their lives."

" Presbyterian? " **I hinted.**

" Narrow gauge, eh? " said the Brakeman; " pretty track; straight as **a** rule; **tunnel** right through the heart **of** a mountain rather than go around it; spirit level grade; strict **rules,** too; passengers have **to** show their tickets before they get **on the train; cars a** little **bit** narrow for sleepers; have to sit one **in a** seat and no room in the aisle **to** dance. No stop-over tickets allowed; passenger must **go** straight through **to the** station he's **tick-**

cted for, or stay off the car. When the car's full, gates are shut; cars built at the shops to hold just so many, and no more allowed on. That road is run right up to the rules and you don't often hear of an accident on it. Had a head-on collision at Schenectady union station and run over a weak bridge at Cincinnati, not many years ago, but nobody hurt, and no passengers lost. Great road."

" May be you rode with the Agnostics? " I tried.

The Brakeman shook his head emphatically.

" Scrub road," he said, " dirt road-bed and no ballast; no time-card, and no train dispatcher. All trains run wild and every engineer makes his own time, just as he pleases. A sort of ' smoke-if-you-want-to ' road. Too many side tracks; every switch wide open all the time, switchman sound asleep and the target-lamp dead out. Get on where you please and get off when you want. Don't have to show your tickets, and the conductor has no authority to collect fare. No, sir; I was offered a pass, but I don't like

the line. I don't care to travel over a road
that has no terminus.

Do you know, I asked a division superintendent where his road run to, and he said
he hoped to die if he knew. I asked him
if the general superintendent could tell me,
and he said he didn't believe they had a
general superintendent, and if they had,
he didn't know any more about the road
than the passengers did. I asked him who
he reported to, and he said, " Nobody." I
asked a conductor who he got his orders
from, and he said he didn't take no orders
from any living man or dead ghost. And
when I asked the engineer who gave him
orders, he said he'd just like to see any
man on this planet try to give him orders,
black-and-white or verbal; he said he'd run
that train to suit himself or he'd run it into
the ditch. Now, you see, I'm not much of
a theologian, but I'm a good deal of a railroad man, and I don't want to run on a road
that has no schedule, makes no time, has no
connections, starts anywhere and runs nowhere, and has neither signal man, train dis-

patcher or superintendent. Might be all right, but I've railroaded too long to understand it."

"Did you try the Methodist?"

"Now you're shoutin'!" he cried with enthusiasm; "that's the hummer! Fast time and crowds of passengers! Engines carry a power of steam, and don't you forget it. Steam-gauge shows a hundred and enough all the time. Lively train crews, too. When the conductor shouts 'All a-b-o-a-r-d!' you can hear him to the next hallelujah station. Every train lamp shines like a head-light. Stop-over privileges on all tickets; passenger can drop off the train any time he pleases, do the station a couple of days and hop on to the next revival train that comes thundering along with an evangelist at the throttle. Good, whole-souled, companionable conductors; ain't a road on earth that makes the passengers feel more at home. No passes issued on any account; everybody pays full traffic rate for his own ticket. Safe road, too; well equipped; Wesleyanhouse air brakes on every train. It's a road I'm fond of, but I didn't begin this week's run with it."

I began to feel that I was running ashore; I tried one more lead:

" May be you went with the Baptists?"

"Ah, ha!" he shouted, " now you're on the Shore line! River Road, eh? Beautiful curves, lines of grace at every bend and sweep of the river; all steel rail and rock ballast; single track, and not a siding from the round-house to the terminus. Takes a heap of water to run it, though; double tanks at every station, and there isn't an engine in the shops that can run a mile or pull a pound with less than two gauges. Runs through a lovely country—river on one side and the hills on the other; and it's a steady climb, up grade all the way until the run ends where the river begins, at the fountain head. Yes, sir, I'll take the River Road every time for a safe trip, sure connections, good time, and no dust blowing in when you open a window. And yesterday morning, when the conductor came around taking up fares with a little basket punch, I didn't ask him to pass me; I paid my fare like a little Jonah—twenty-five cents for a ninety-minute run, with a concert by the passengers thrown in. I tell you what it is, Pilgrim, never mind your baggage, you just secure your passage on the River Road if you want to go to—"

But just here the long whistle announced a station, and the Brakeman hurried to the door, shouting—

"Zions-VILLE! ZIONS-ville! All out for Zionsville! This train makes no stops between here and Indianapolis!"

# LAUREL AND CYPRESS

## XVI

S a recruit in the Forty-seventh Illinois regiment, and one of the rawest recruits that ever marched against the insolent foe, I had suffered no humiliation from his domineering assurance. I knew that pride is bound in the heart of the foe, and insolence is inherent in him. This arrogance, as a free man, I resented.

I had not been free a very great while. I was but six months out of the Peoria high school, where I had been an abject slave to a horde of tyrants, of both sexes, whom I love unto this day for their gentle tyranny and loving despotism. But now that I was free, I speedily learned that freedom is not

" ―――― as the poet's dream,
  A fair young girl, with light and delicate limbs,
  And wavy tresses gushing from the cap
  With which the Roman master crowned his slaves
  When he took off the gyves.  A bearded man,
  Armed to the teeth "

was he, and we called him " Colonel " for short, and whatsoever he commanded us to do we did, and did it with bewildering alacrity.

Weeks added themselves up into months and I saw no indication of the presence of the remorseless enemy.  I greatly deplored the masterly inactivity of the army, much to the amusement of the old soldiers, who appeared to like it.  I feared the war might close before I got into a battle, and I would go home, with no man's blood upon my hands, disgraced forever.

I took the usual studies in the school of the soldier, all compulsory, and thought of the pleasant discipline of the high school as I wrestled with a musket longer than myself. And alway and all the time, waking or dreaming, I longed for war; grim-visaged war, with arms on armor clashing and all his dogs in full cry. I yearned for battle; I mocked at fear; I prayed for the thunder of the captains and the shouting, and wanted to go on all by myself and meet the armed men.

There came a rainy day in May, away back in '63, when the bugles sang reveille at three o'clock and we marched out of camp in unseemly haste. Splash, splash, splash all day in the rain and Mississippi mud. Much did I envy the "boundless liberty of speech" which prevailed among Xenophon's immortal Ten Thousand, "wrangling with the generals on every new order," and Xenophon himself not above wrangling with privates of the line. But I knew that my Colonel was not Xenophon. I also knew that if I had any criticisms concerning the conduct of the war I had better make them in classic Greek. Wherefore I kept silence, though my bones waxed old with my inward roaring.

It was about midday, I think—dinner was omitted from the bill of fare that day—when

we observed certain signs of restlessness,
luminously intelligible to my comrades and
with the pleasantly exciting interest of a new
problem to myself. The leading company
suddenly left the column, threw down a score
of panels in the rail fence, deployed across the
field and disappeared in the woods on the
double-quick. The silence in the soaking,
patient ranks was broken by a little murmur
of expectation, that rippled into a sparkle of
jest and laughter, as, filing into the field, we
were aligned facing the woods that had so
mysteriously swallowed up the skirmishers.
We waited. Somewhere out of sight, away
down the line, a cannon was booming at sul-
len intervals, accenting the irregular recitative of scattering rifle shots. The Colonel
shouted a command that startled me by its
explosiveness; our muskets rattled to '' right
shoulder shift'' and we marched into the woods.
Here we were ordered to '' load and lie
down.'' To me this smacked of caution so
excessive that it seemed tainted with cow-
ardice. But as that was impossible in such

a regiment, with such a Colonel, I reserved my decision, and asked a sergeant:

" What is it? "

" We are going to have a shindy," he replied, " do you dance? "

Before I could reply that I did feel a little supple in the knee joints, another man said " he didn't believe there would be much of a fight." I observed that only recruits like myself spoke of "battles." I was not afraid, indeed there was nothing to be afraid of, but there was a little catch in my breath I could neither understand nor control. It was rather hard to draw a deep, lung-filling inhalation. There was a continuous chatter of all manner of nonsense along the line, a great deal of ill-timed levity, a painful amount of unnecessary profanity jarring back and forth. All this frivolity rasped across my feelings; I was nervously irritated by it.

It appeared to me, from all I could gather, that we were on the eve of a very solemn occasion, and a brief season of prayer would be more appropriate than all this flippant, not to say irreverent, badinage and repartee. While thus communing with myself, a staff officer drew rein in our front, and, in a few ill-chosen words, delivered the most irreligious exhortation to which I had ever listened. A few minutes after he disappeared, however, the general himself rode along the line, and his perfervid denunciation of the enemy and extravagant laudation of our single-handed ability to whip all creation, made lurid by picturesque and polysyllabic profanity, convinced me that the officer whom I had mistaken for a godless aide was only a cavalry chaplain off duty.

Being a recruit, and not knowing very much about battles, I was determined to see this one. Scorning to shelter myself, I stood up. When sternly ordered to lie down, I merely half obeyed and sat up, stretching my short neck to its utmost tension and straining my eyes to see what was going on. There was nothing on earth to make one afraid. I was painfully disappointed, fearing that after all this was a false alarm and there would be no battle. Certainly it did not start out like the battles in the books and the war stories.

What there was to see, I could see. Every
faculty was abnormally alert. I saw the skirmish lines down in the valley that spread
out below us. I heard Worthington say,
"Haven't those fellows got a splendid line?"
And indeed the men in gray were doing a
beautiful skirmish drill. Puff, puff, puff—
the little clouds of smoke broke out from the
gray line in the mist, and the muffled shots
came bluntly through the non-resonant air.
I saw a soldier fall on his face, as the blue-
bloused skirmish line moved steadily forward,
but not until I observed that he did not rise
to his feet and go on with his comrades did I
realize that he had not merely stumbled.
Even then, he was so far away, it seemed as
though I was looking at a picture, or that I
had read about all this in some old history.
I saw the skirmishers suddenly rush together
in little groups—and again deploy as quickly.
I saw them run forward and dart back. I
saw an orderly riding hard to the front with
a box of cartridges on his saddle-bow. I
wondered why they didn't begin the battle.
I was waiting to see the long line of gleaming

bayonets, with the Colonel in the lead, sweep across the open field, impaling the writhing enemy on the glittering points of steel. I waited a long, long time before I saw anything like that.

A tall man in gray uniform, wearing a Spanish beard, came over the brow of the wooded hill, and half halted as he came suddenly in sight of our line. A chorus of jeers and taunts greeted him. He gravely saluted the Colonel, and smilingly replied to a general inquiry from the soldiers as to the health of his command:

"I reckon you-all will find some that's harder to catch than me before you-all get into Jackson."

Then a soldier rose up and escorted him through our ranks to the rear. We had taken a prisoner, anyhow; an officer, at that. It was beginning to look a little bit like war. My soaking uniform was uncomfortable; I eased a chafing cross-belt. There was grit in one of my shoes that annoyed me, but when I bent to untie the shoe-string, the soggy leather was so clammy and muddy

that it discouraged me, and I decided to wait
till we went into camp. I was hungry. I
felt in my haversack. It was empty. Some
one laughed at my rueful face as I shook the
crumbs from my flabby commissariat. I had
eaten my breakfast, dinner and supper on the
march.

Just at our left the Waterhouse battery went
into position; the guns without loss of time
began thundering away at the enemy with
cheery energy. That was like "sure enough"
war, and roused me from my momentary list-
lessness. For I must confess that even the
prisoner had disappointed me a little, because
he didn't seem to mind it very much. I
stood up to watch the gunners at work. A
spent bullet came whining along and angrily
knocked a handful of bark from the tree
against which I leaned.

" See that!" said a sergeant; " better lie
down and let the tree stop the next one, too.
It'll do it as well as your head; may be better."

I sat down again, but not very profoundly

impressed. By and by the battery ceased firing.

"They are letting the guns cool," a soldier said.

"They are going to let us get out of this," said some one else.

I turned again to look at the battery. Half seated on the hub of a cannon wheel lounged a young fellow not much older than myself, but much taller. Nineteen or twenty he may have been. His jacket, with its red trimming, was closely buttoned. He laid his arm on a spoke of the wheel, and rested his cheek on the palm of his hand. He was tired, but his breathing was deep and even. As he sat there, a handsome boy, looking out through the rain and mist, the far away look in his eyes seemed to be resting on something a thousand miles away from those shifting skirmish lines playing tag with each other on the rain-soaked meadow.

A sound, such as I had never heard in all my life, struck upon my ear and heart with a horror that turned me faint. The artillery-man threw his right hand quickly to his

215

breast and swayed slowly forward, clinging to the wheel with his left hand, while his sudden cry, quivering with **pain,** thrilled down the line like an arrow—

"Murder! Oh, murder, boys! Murder!"

One **of his** comrades sprang to catch him, but his weak grasp on the wheel relaxed, **his** hand slipped away and he lay on the trampled grass, the soft rain beating in his face, a **red** stain widening under his wet hand and oozing out between those clutching fingers. His cry was not repeated; it faded **away** into weak, **gasping** moans that made me wince as though they were **knife** thrusts. Some musicians, with the white badges on their sleeves, came hurrying up with the stretcher. I watched them lift the moaning cannoneer upon it and start back with him to where the yellow **flag** hung limp above the field hospital. Fear, **be**-fore unknown, came leaping into my heart with that hissing, spiteful bullet. That which I had wanted **to** see, which I had longed to see, which **I** had dreaded lest **I** might miss see**ing,** had sprung into the light before my eyes, **and I** was sick and faint.

*The young artillery-man threw his right hand quickly to his breast and swayed slowly forward, while his sudden cry, quivering with pain, thrilled down the line like an arrow.*　(Page 216.)

Nerveless, with flaccid muscles relaxed, I shrank down to the ground, fairly burrowing my face in the grass to shut out these things that had so suddenly taken on new and terrible meaning. Hideous things; unseen and deadly; a destruction that wasted at noon-day, viewless as the pestilence that walketh in darkness. With all the fortitude and strength of will I could rally, I nerved myself to keep from trembling. Mechanically I laid my hand upon the rifle at my side and shuddered at the chilling touch of the steel barrel, now that I knew so well what lay sleeping in its dark chamber. I wondered if I could have the courage, the very daring to awaken the cruel force I had so eagerly thrust into it when Lieutenant Law said, "Load at will." Did the lieutenant know what he was saying? By and by Captain McClure would say:

"Fire!"

And then?

Came back, like an answer to the question, the thrilling cry of the wounded gunner:

"Murder! Murder!"

I did not know—may be it was another boy
—a school-boy, too—who, not seeing the
Federal artilleryman, had killed him. The
boy who fired that shot—why, the war was
scarce a year old—his mother's kisses were
yet warm on his cheek and lip. His sister's
arms but yesterday unwound their caressing
clasp from his neck. Such a warm-hearted,
loving boy, they would tell you. Tender-
hearted as a girl; he had never done a cruel
deed in his life. From the days when first
he lisped his prayers at his mother's knees,
morning and evening he had knelt to the
Prince of Peace and prayed that his heart
might be kept pure and gentle, free from the
taint of sin.

And now?

See what he had done! With no reason
for hating him, he had killed this boy from
the Northland. He had committed a sin so
far away from all his boyish thought that it
may be he had never prayed against it. He
had dipped the hand that his mother loved to
feel on her face into the blood of his brother!

And this boy whom he had killed—he, too,

218

was a good boy, loving and kind-hearted. His mother had kissed him good-bye in that far-away Illinois home, with her tears raining through her kisses, just as the rain of May fell upon the white, pain-drawn face of her boy a little minute ago. His sister had sobbed her good-bye in his arms, holding him close against the heart that had loved him from babyhood, and now would break for him. A quiet, gentle, loving boy. Always, they would tell you, there was laughter in his eyes; always his voice was soft, and sweet as a woman's—ah, they never heard him cry out as I did, just now! And he, too, morning and evening, knelt down with bowed head and clasped hands, and his petitions, ascending to the throne of Infinite Love, mingled there with the prayers of that boy in Alabama.

What friends, what loyal, true-hearted friends, those boys had been had they met some time other than that gray, sunless day in May. And yet, not an hour ago, the boy from Illinois was working at that murderous gun like a blacksmith at his forge. When

with fierce breath **of flame** it **roared out
its** horrid message **of** pitiless defiance, **how**
that white-handed boy sprang with his sponge
staff **to** wipe the black powder stains from its
**grim** lips, and cool the rifled throat, hot with
hate. **How** proudly he patted its sides of
bronze when it landed a screaming shell **into**
a group of men and boys on the farther side
**of** the meadow. And then, sitting there on
the hub of the wheel, **the** rage **of** battle **in** his
heart subsiding even as **the** gun cooled **at his**
side, that home-longing **look came into his
eyes,** his soul drifted away to a home on the
**shore of Lake** Michigan; his mother and sister were **in** his thought—

And **a boy not** unlike himself, standing in
a little clump **of** blossoming bushes that
fringed the meadow brook, slowly raised his
rifle to his shoulder, aimed at **a** cloud of white
smoke drifting away from the last shot of that
terrible gun, and, without seeing who **was** sitting behind that beautiful screen, fired, **and**
killed **a** boy to whom **his** soul might have
knitted itself, **as the soul of** Jonathan clave
unto David.

"Murder! Oh, murder, boys!"

Well for the boy in the Southland that he could not hear that cry. And well for our boys in all our land if they shall never hear it. Better still if they shall never call it into shrill condemning life from blood-flecked lips.

A bugle call dropping into the momentary silence that punctuated the skirmishing, a clatter of hoof-beats on the sodden turf, a phantom of mounted men sweeping past the colors in the mist; the guns are hurriedly limbering up; the Colonel's voice translates the bugle song in a ringing shout; a rush of men leaping to their feet; a quick march forward for a few hundred paces; then the step quickens into a run; a mad, wild rush down the wooded hillside; a confronting line of gray waiting for us in the valley; cheer after cheer breaking into the storm of the charge like the combing waves on a rocky shore; the guns thundering over our heads, volleys of musketry that roll away to right and left, rattling back to repeat themselves again; the gray line breaking before our onset, flying like scattering clouds before a swift north wind; splashing down into the yellow stream, rain-swollen and muddy, climbing up the slippery banks, scrambling over the breast-works; every man a hero in the madness and tempest of the charge, while Fear lags far behind in the confusion at the rear; cheering and more cheering; laughter and shouting; wounded men waving their caps from the stretchers, or feebly lifting their heads as they lie on the ground, raising their pain-broken voices to cheer with us—hurrah! hurrah! And again hurrah! Every jubilant sound that exultation can invent and make—hurrah! Then we catch breath from our shouting and hurry away to hunt out the refugees and cor-ral our prisoners.

Midnight, and we were bivouacked in the square of the state-house in Jackson. The rainy day, the muddy marching, and the hard fighting were things of the past. My brain was in a whirl over my first battle. I opened my eyes and vainly tried to recall it all in de-tail. Then I resolutely closed them and tried to sleep. I thought over a letter I would write home; wild with a sense of victory and proud, oh! so immeasurably proud that I had some little part in it. Sighing at last in the very excess of pride and delight, and again closing my eyes tight, tight, as a child will do, and earnestly saying, " Now I will go to sleep." And then I whispered a prayer I had forgotten all through the peril and fear of the day, and looked my good-night up at the stars.

Calm ; silent ; tranquil. Undimmed by all the smoke and blood of the battle-field. Unshaken by the tumult of thundering guns and charging battalions, each in its place, the unchanged and unchanging constellations looked down upon the little world in which men lived and slept ; loved and hated ; fought and died. The quiet, peaceful, blessed starlight.

My thoughts went northward over southern meadows and rushing streams to a little home by Peoria lake, where a mother and sisters waited for me. Slowly they came back again to the battery in action on the brow of the wooded hill ; with a troubled mind I wondered how long mother and sister might wait. I laid my arm across my eyes to shut out something that dimmed the starlight and the victory with the stain that marred the first altar of prayer and sacrifice. I tried to shut out all the muffled sounds of the guarded bivouac, and, by and by, I fell asleep. And still, in the flush of triumph, in the radiant hope of victories yet to come, and honors to be won on other fields, dropped into my restless sleep and troubled dreams that fainting cry under the wheels of the gun,

"Murder! Oh, murder, boys! Murder!"

# THE LEGEND OF THE GOOD DRUMMUH

## XVII

OW it was in the reign of the good Caliph—may his memory be sweet—when all the land was blooming and fruitful; when every man was a daisy and every girl a peach; when ten buyers laid hold of one seller, and to be a Drummuh was greater than a king; when the bulbul sang in the meadows and made it lively for the picnic from the city when it camped upon his claim; when the caravans went up and down the trail, and the side-show blower rasped the echoes of Reubenville with his strident voice—that Abou Ben Evrawhair came to the city of Mhrahaha in the land of Ohoho. Straight-

15                    225

way he hied himself to the caravanserai, which is called the Phœnix House, because that daily it is new-risen from its hashes. He flung his grip upon the counter, wrote his name all over the register, spake unto the clark imperiously, and said:

"A sample-room on the parlor floor, put in a fire, send my trunks up right away, order me a livery rig, get me a messenger and see that thou call me for the 6:38 A. M. east without fail."

But Seme Taik Munnica the Clark looked not at him, neither answered him aught, but walked slowly to the mirror and gazed upon himself, for he was well-favored and fair to look upon. And he himself knew it.

And Abou Ben Evrawhair gat him forth from the caravanserai, for he was an hustler, and he went into the booths and bazars of the merchants and them that sell, and he laid hold upon them and held them up, and he filled them to overflowing with new stories and marvelous incidents by flood and field, and he wrote down orders which they gave

226

not while they laughed, and got upon them the cinch of the good salesman.

And them that were obstinate enticed he unto his room, and spread out his samples before them until that they were bewildered and knew not what they lacked nor what they wanted, and to these he sold the biggest bills. For Abou Ben Evrawhair had sand, which was also salted with gall; he stropped his razor on his cheek and shaved the other man with it. Moreover he slept not in the day-time, neither was he dormant during business hours. Likewise he was exceeding broad between the eyes, and from his frontal bone to his occiput it was a long way for a slow man. And because that his head was his capital he carried it level, for he said, "A drinking man can't even sell whisky."

And when even was come he gat him to bed and slept. For he said: "It is a dead town and there is no place to go."

And before the second watch of the night Rhumul em Uhp the Porter smote on the panels of his door and cried aloud:

"Oh, Abou Ben Evrawhair, arise and

dress! The day stayeth not and thy **train is** on time and coming right along!''

**A**nd Abou Ben Evrawhair arose and girt his **raiment** about him blindly, and he marveled that he was so sleepy, for he knew that he went **to** bed exceeding early, even with the fowls of the barn-yard.

And when they reached the station, **lo, it** was the mail train west, and it was 10 : 25 P. M.

And Abou Ben Evrawhair reached **for** Rhumul em Uhp **the** Porter and caught him **a** half-arm jab **in the** neck, **and he said** unto him :

''**Carry** me back **to** my room and pay **thou** the 'bus **man** both ways, for I will **not. And** see that thou call me at 6: 38 A. M. **or thou** shalt die the death.''

And he gat himself up into his bed, which was even a corn-cob mattress laid **on basswood** slats, **but he** recked not, **for his busy** day made his sleep sweet.

And **at** the midnight **watch it was so that** Rhumul **em** Uhp the Porter beat again upon his door and shouted so that all the corridor might hear :

. . . "*The hour is late, the way is long and the 'bus runneth not for this train.*"  (Page 280.)

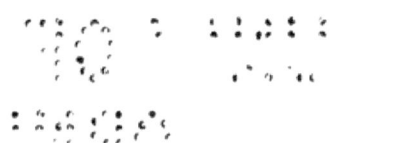

"Awake, Abou Ben Evrawhair, thou of the long reach and short temper, for the time waneth and the train stayeth for no man! Awake, and haste! For slumber overtook thy servant, the hour is late, the way is long, and the 'bus runneth not for this train!"

And Abou Ben Evrawhair arose and cast on his garments as one loadeth hay, and girded up his loins, and gat forth with great speed, for his heart was anxious. Nevertheless he gave Rhumul em Uhp a shekel of silver and bade him carry his two grips, and railed upon him for a driveling laggard.

And when they were come to the station, behold, it was 11 : 46 P. M., and the train was a way freight going south.

And Abou Ben Evrawhair fell upon Rhumul em Uhp the Porter and out-classed him, though he was under his weight; and he smote him sore and entreated him roughly, and said:

"Oh, pale gray ass of all asses! the prophet pity thee if thou call me once more before 6: 38 A. M."

And he walked back to his inn and gat

229

him to bed. And sleep fell upon him heavily, for he was sore discouraged, and he said within himself, " Is this a business trip or a six-days walking match?"

And when he was in the soundest of his slumber, it was so that Rhumul em Uhp the Porter kicked fiercely against his door with a noise that would call the Seven of Ephesus. And he cried through the transom,

" Oh, Abou Ben Evrawhair, Prince of Drummuhs! May thy sleep be sweet! Awake and dress with speed! It is night in the valleys, but the day star shines upon the mountains. Truly thy train is even now due at the station, but the 'bus is indeed gone!"

And Abou Ben Evrawhair the Drummuh frightened himself awake, for he said, " If I lose that train I am out a good customer!" And he stayed not to tie his shoes, but put on his garments as he ran to the station, while Rhumul em Uhp the Porter splashed ahead with one grip and a lantern.

For it was pitch dark, knee deep, and raining like a house-a-fire.

230

And when they reached the station, Rhumul em Uhp the Porter cried aloud and said:

"May the Profit prosper thy samples, O
Abou Ben Evrawhair, favored of Fate! For
verily I am a hustler, thou art a lucky man,
and thy train still waiteth for thee!"

And, lo, it was a gravel train, going west
the next morning, and the clock in the steeple
tolled 2 A. M.

And Abou Ben Evrawhair stood up before
Rhumul em Uhp the Porter. And he caught
him by the beard and fanned him with his
boots, and beat him and pelted him with mud
and words all the way back to the kahn.
And he seized his lantern from him and
smashed it over the head of the wooden In-
dian in front of Kabbijleef, the Tobacconist's.
And he wept with rage, and said:

"Would that I owned the Phœnix House!
For then would I slay thee and hire this grav-
en image in thy place, O thou that art swift
to blunder! Only art thou fit to stand in the
post-office and hold out thy tongue for men
to lick stamps thereon!"

And he was red-hot. So that when the

watchman of the night bade him hold his peace, Abou Ben Evrawhair was rejoiced to be sassed, for he ached to relieve himself. And he lifted up his voice still louder, and he blessed the watchman with the left-handed blessing of the tribe of the Gamins, and he called him a Cop, and pushed him out from the shelter of the awning, even into the rain, and wet his new uniform.

For Abou Ben Evrawhair, of the tribe of Roun da Boutoun, had seen watchmen of many cities, and he feared nothing in all the world save a slick customer.

And when they reached the caravanserai he repeated his order and gat him to bed once more.

Now, when Abou Ben Evrawhair awoke the next time, he called himself. And the sun was high and shone in at his windows; and the noise of the trolley and the chariots of the merchant rattled in the street.

And his heart sank within him, for his watch had stopped. Wherefore he girt his garments on him and went softly down stairs, for he was dumb with fear.

And Seme Taik Munnica the Clark, which was behind the counter, greeted him, and said:

"O Abou Ben Evrawhair, live in peace! It is too late for breakfast and too early for dinner. Nevertheless, it shall not make any difference in the bill."

But Abou Ben Evrawhair could not speak, for he was voiceless with wrath. And when he had pulled himself together he sought out Rhumul em Uhp the Porter, and he said unto him:

"O Chuck el edded Pup" (which is, thou that sleepest at train time), "wherefore hast thou forgotten to call me?"

And Rhumul em Uhp was for the first time angry, and he spread out his hands and cried:

"O Abou Ben Evrawhair the Drummuh, quick in speech and hasty to slug without cause! Wherefore shouldest thou get up at day-break when there is another train goeth the same way at the same hour to-morrow morning? Wilt thou also join thyself unto the tribe of Kickahs?"

233

For the Kickahs are a people abhorred of them who dwell in the kahns.

And Abou Ben Evrawhair tore his hair and rent his garments, and cried:

"Woe is me, for am I not stuck in this dead town another day?"

But Rhumul em Uhp the Porter mocked him and said:

"Manana!"

For he had learned to swear in New Mexico.

And Abou Ben Evrawhair would not hearken unto the people of the kahn. But he paid his bill, and hired a man and a team to take him to the next town, which was the village of Wayback, on the Dead Branch of the Dry Fork of Lost Creek. Neither did any merchant dwell therein.

And Abou Ben Evrawhair mocked Seme Taik Munnica the Clark; neither would he further patronize the house, but he hired his team from a livery stable down the street.

Now, the livery stable belonged to the house, all the same. But Abou Ben Evra-

234

whair, which was the son of Noah Bout Evrathing, wist not that it was so.

For of a truth no man can know everything unless he had settled on this planet before the surveyor's stakes were set, and hath never been away from it since.

# HOUSEHOLD PETS

## XVIII

ANEM virumque cano. Some-
times I cano them to my grief.
Pardon the little touch of clas-
sical reminiscence with which
this brochure opens; it is an
old man's weakness and privilege to quote
these broken scraps of bookish lore that cling
to his memory, barnacles that fastened themselves to his bark, not to say bight, in the
early days of his school-boy voyages out
into the wide, wide sea of knowledge. And
the hereinbefore quotation is all that remains
to me of Virgil's Æneid and Geraint, or,
more properly speaking, Gerisn't. But what
recks it? The captain, usually, or else the
pilot.

In common with the majority of good men,

I like dogs. I can not say that I love man's faithful friend. I reserve my love for my human friends. I do not care to have even a good dog, as good as my neighbor is apt to own, sit at the table and dine with me. I do not enjoy having a long-haired dog with dewclaws, in bed with me. I prefer to sleep in "fearful solitude," rather than share my couch with the best dog that ever dug rats from under a hen-house. I am not partial to dogs in the parlor.

Being naturally a cold, undemonstrative man, I am apt to be repellent rather than effusively cordial when, on a sultry July day, a hairy dog, with an undergrowth of furry pin-feathers, weighing 108 pounds, coming in out of the rain with an ancient and a fish-like smell, climbs into my lap and endeavors to lave my resisting face with a moist tongue eleven and one-half inches long. I know that I have sorely grieved some of my friends by coldly rejecting the cordial advances of their dogs, but I can not help this formal demeanor on my part toward dogs with whom I am but slightly acquainted.

237

I am so constituted, by transmitted heredity and the influence of environment, that I can not endure to have a high-bred dog which, or perhaps I had better say whom, I have just seen shaking and hauling a plebeian pig by the ear, or carrying a long-abandoned bone to his lair, leave his quarry and extend his prehensile tongue to salute my shrinking cheek.

I am aware that I am prudish, and morbidly over-sensitive on this subject; people who live with dogs have told me so; but I can not help it. True, there are dogs which —or, again, shall I say who?—never touch anything that is offensive or unclean under the law; I know this, because the dog's master has told me so himself. But I am an old man, and in the course of my long life I have met so many liars of various kinds that I am sometimes troubled by a haunting fear that even a good man, led away by his loving partiality, might at times be tempted to make misleading statements concerning the habits and sagacity of the dog of his heart.

And yet I was not always thus, a savage

foe of still more savage dogs. When I was a boy, every homeless dog that wandered into our neighborhood knew me for his friend, followed me home, shared my meals, destroyed our garden, and made things lively for the poultry. I still maintain that it is the inalienable right of every boy to own a dog; as many dogs, indeed, as his father's income and good-nature will permit. It is the full-grown man whose dog makes me tired.

The man always takes it for granted that you love his dog as you love him. Well, sometimes this is true. But, in such a case, it does not augur well for the man. Not that I love Cæsar more, but that I love his master less.

There was a time, in happy days gone by, when I sat under my own vine and fig tree and smoked the pipe of peace—the only pipe I can smoke without contracting *mal de mer*—in harmony with all mankind, and fondly watched my garden grow, for I am a lover of things that grow out of doors and stay where you put them. At times a friend sat at my side, and as we whiled away the hours in

239

sweet converse his playful dog would gam-
bol with his fellows—my other friends' equally
playful dogs—upon the lawn.

I kept no dog myself; I couldn't afford it;
it was all I could do to maintain a dormitory
and campus for the neighbors' dogs, so I self-
fishly reaped my enjoyment of dog-life from
the merry antics of the dogs of my friends. A
smooth shaven lawn, in all the delicate health
of its teething year, with a seventy-four pound
dog creating an earth-geyser in the middle of
it, as he burrows his excited way Chinawards,
presents a spectacle that leaves an impression
upon the mind of the man who plays the
lawn-mower in his own open air concerts that
lasts long, long after all love for the dog has
died out of his heart.

My friend looks at the dog with eyes that
sparkle with admiration.

"He's the greatest dog to dig," says he.

"Is he?" I ask with an interested inflection and heavy accent on the "is," as though
I didn't know it, but hoped it might be true.

"Land, yes," says Amicus, " he'll have a

hole in your lawn that you can bury a cow in before he gets through."

I say, "Will he?" with waning enthusiasm, **and think** within myself that **if** he will just **stop** when he gets **a** hole deep enough **to** bury **a** dog **in, it will** answer my purpose quite as well, **as** I have **no** cow which I **wish** to bury. But before **he** gets **it** quite deep enough something discourages him, **and he** wanders **about the lawn** prospecting in different **ent** places.

"Ha, ha! now look **at them,"** remarks another **friend, upon** another occasion, **as** four dogs of **three** friends, ceasing to dig in **five** quarters of the reservation, open a free-for-all wrestling match in the heart of a flower-bed—"look **at them!** That brindle dog of **mine is** as strong **as a** bull."

"Is he?" I ask **again** with the well simulated expression of interested innocence.

"Yes, **indeed; he'd** pull down **a** lion. See him worry Thornton's big dog over that rose bush. He's only a pup, **too.** That fellow's only **ten** months old."

I think, by the way he tears and tramples

and crushes things, that he must be a century old at least, but I only say:

"Oh!"

The English language is not, as some philologists have declared, a meager, inexpressive, poverty-stricken tongue. It is rich; rich beyond measure in its delicate shadings of meaning. One can hardly estimate how many volumes a man may speak when he says but "Oh." So I merely said, "Oh!" with the circumflex accent on the "Oh."

All dogs are not diggers. Dogs—at least the dogs of my friends, have gifts differing according to the spirit of destruction that is given them. Some of these dogs whom I have known were racers, and in the early summers of my lawn these did so run that they wore a deep, broad path around the house, hard as a floor of brick, whereon would grow no living thing, not even plantain, with tangent paths leading to the sally ports by which they left the Præsidio when I shot at them from my upper windows with a Flobert rifle.

And some were gnawers, and these gnawed

the piazza posts, the hammock, the young trees, books, umbrellas, canes, door-mats, garden seats—any thing they could find out of doors, and tried to get into the house for more. Some again were cat-hunters, *Canis felinus*, and these slew Robbie's kittens, three in succession, causing the owner of the kittens deep childish grief, which led the masters of the dogs to remark, after the carnage, that "he was the boss dog for cats; you must keep your cats shut up when (Bismarck, Terror, Avenger) comes around."

I meekly said I would do so, hereafter, which promise I could safely make, as my stock of cats, old and juvenile, was exhausted. This did not bring quiet, however, because Bismarck, Terror, Avenger, *et als*, deprived of their natural sources of amusement, made vigorous search for additional material, and prowled around the house and barn digging, gnawing and scratching. I think my friends felt a little hurt at this, and believed that I had meanly concealed or sent away the remnant of cats that was left in order to deprive their dogs of a little innocent pleasure. In

243

vain I assured them that I was entirely out of cats. My friends looked incredulous, and said:

"It is very strange; very strange. I never knew that dog of mine to be mistaken about cats. By the way he acts there surely must be a cat somewhere about the place."

I felt so grieved by these unjust suspicions that I went so far as to buy a cat for my friends' dogs to play with. And I went to no little trouble to get a good one; one that would please them. I do not know much about cats, so I acted on the judgment of a young man named Connors, Mr. William Connors, who lives in a sailors' lodging-house down near the wharf, to whom I had a letter of introduction from an acquaintance in the sporting line. "Ratty Connors," the neighbors called Mr. William. He sold me a brindled cat with but one eye and a fragmentary tail. Mr. Connors told me the cat was a pet of his little girl who died, and it broke his heart to look at her, otherwise money could not buy her. She was gentle as a dove, he said. Her name was Celeste.

I carried the "gentle cat" home in a bird cage. She got one paw through the wires and struck the conductor in the leg as he passed my seat, as I journeyed out of the city. He came back, after he had taken up the tickets, and told me I must take that mole trap into the baggage car.

When I got home, a friend was sitting on my piazza watching his dog—a Digger—at play in a pansy bed. I said:

"I have brought home a little play-fellow for Excavator."

I then turned Celeste loose; she made for the half buried Digger, as stoops the hawk upon the prey, hauled him out of his hole, swept her claws across his howling face like a besom of destruction, and made life a burden to him before they had been acquainted five minutes. When the dog was too tired to play any longer, Celeste shrieked in a weird, uncanny manner, and went away, and I never saw her again.

The next day, however, a friend who owned a cat-dog, told me that early in the preceding evening, an Alleghany mountain wild cat came into his yard, fell upon Avenger, tore the **face off** him like a mask, and otherwise **so** lacerated and cat-handled him **that** next morning the sight **of a** little kitten, **no** bigger than a mole, scared him **so** that he ran half way **up** the side of **a** two-story barn, before he knew where he was going. I didn't say anything about Celeste, because, when I wondered that there should **be wild** cats infesting the lawns of suburban Philadelphia, the man grew very angry and **offered to** go before **a justice of** the **peace and make** affidavit **to it.** So, **for the** sake **of peace, I** said **I** believed him.

**If** I believed one-half **of** one-tenth **of the** things I tell people I do, my creed, measuring thirty-nine articles to the **foot, would** reach from here to the moon.

I have always been afraid that Mr. **Connors** deceived me about that cat.

**Some of** the dogs of **my** friends were Sleepers, *Canis somnolentus*. These would sneak **into** the house and crawl under the sofa **or** climb upon the best beds in the house, **and**

slumber, and play tag with the pillow shams, and pursue the elusive flea over their persons.

There appears to be a strong *esprit de corps* among fleas. I have ever noticed that fleas from different dogs never agreed with the human persons to whom they emigrated.

By nature, I am not a revengeful man. The few murders I have committed, in the course of a wild and wandering career, when I have had abundant opportunities to commit many more, were not the outgrowth of cold premeditation and a tigerish desire for blood. My massacres were in the strict line of duty as a war correspondent, and they were not congenial to me.

Many a time have I risen from my desk, my soul sick of carnage, and reeled away to wash my dripping pen at the nearest pump, feeling that if the paper required any more slaughter on the next day, it would have to hire a new man to do its butchery. I have ever maintained that it is the business of the armies in the field to do the killing, and that some combatant, other than the war correspondent, should expose himself to death, and strew the gory field with ghastly heaps of slain. But **no**; under our artificial civilization, **all** this the correspondent has **to do** himself. "Take away the sword; armies can be destroyed without it."

But while **I am a** peace-loving, forgiving man, near the close of the summer to which I have referred, I bought a young cow. She was a callow, timid young thing; somewhat shy, and rather giddy, **as a cow is apt** to be in that sweet caramel time of life. Her **voice was** changing, **and when** she ran sideways a few steps, twisted her tail **in a very** unladylike manner, **and** tried **to** sing, she gave utterance **to** the **most** extraordinary tones that ever startled an inexperienced cow-herd. But **with** all her foolish little affectations, she was good-hearted, and I made allowance for **the** inevitable silliness **of** her first season. She **had a** mild Jersey **eye and a Texas** appetite.

One evening I called **on one of my friends** to enjoy the **sunset from** his piazza. He **is a very** wealthy man, who had the sun set on the western **side of** his house, because he said

248

that was so much the pleasanter side in the evening. He said the morning sun shone on the east piazza, which would make it very disagreeable if one had to view the sunset from that side. Ah, me! what a priceless boon is wealth. Now, I am not able to command such luxuries, consequently the sun sets all around my house, wherever it pleases, like a hen.

When I made this call I took Joshua, the cow, with me. I call her Joshua because she is the son of none. She was very reluctant to lead, and had me on several sides of the road four or five times as we sauntered along in the level rays of the declining sun. I forget what it was declining, but it was very red in the face. When we reached our friend's house, I was glad to sit down and tie Joshua to a cast-iron dog on the piazza. My friend is very fond of sculpture, and once told me that he had picked up that dog at an art sale for seven dollars. He thinks it is certainly an old master, as he can find no one who can tell him who sculptured it.

The family seemed surprised to see Joshua with me, but I said:

"Oh, love me, love my cow, you know. I couldn't get away without her. We are inseparables. That cow has more sense than most men. She watches for me when I am away, and when she sees me coming there is something touching in her demonstrations of affectionate welcome. No matter how tired or sick she may be, she always runs to meet me. Wherever I go she goes; doesn't she, girlie?"

I had never heard this said about a cow, but many times had it given to me about dogs, so I said my piece pretty well. When I finished, Joshua stood on her hands and trilled a stave from the drinking chorus in "Meyerbeer," and all the people shrank back a little, while the cast-iron dog turned pale.

"She's great on that," I said, enthusiastically. "I never yet saw a cow who could stand in the same pasture with her on that hand-spring trick."

"It's a little rough on a man's lawn,

though," my friend said, looking sadly at Joshua's hoof prints in the velvet grass.

" Oh," I said proudly, " that's nothing. Just wait a few minutes until she begins to feel at home and bucks. She feels a little strange now, of course," I added, sympathetically, " but when she gets used to all these strange faces, and feels good, she'll jump up about eight feet in the air, come down with her four hoofs so close together you could cover them with a lady's handkerchief, then she'll just spread them and tear up more sod in one scratch than you can put back in a week."

At that moment a nurse-maid came along wheeling a little cab with a sweet little baby therein. Joshua fired out her hind leg, knocked the top off the cab, upset the nurse and raised Bedlam on the piazza.

" My child! my child!" shrieked the mother. But the baby wasn't hurt, and by and by things quieted down a little. I said that Donna didn't like babies and they'd better keep their children in the house when she came with me. " She's a whole league nine to kick,'' I said. '' I call her Prima Donna because she's such a kicker.''

My friend didn't say anything, and I felt afraid that he was a little touched with envy. So I rose to go. Just then Prima Donna bucked high in the air, jerking the '' Old Master '' from his perch on the piazza. This frightened her, and she bolted, and away they went, Militia—I call her Militia because she's such a good runner—and the iron dog; over the lawn, through the flower beds, down the gravel walks, around the house, the iron dog bouncing and jumping like a thing of life. I laughed till I cried.

'' I never saw her in such spirits,'' I said. '' Just wait until she sees Bismarck!''

My friend did not reply. He was crying as much as I was, but I don't think he was laughing so heartily. At that instant Luna— I call her Luna because she comes on tied so often—saw Bismarck, the cat-dog. With one jump she broke the leg off the iron dog, reached Bismarck in a single bound, and with a little coquettish play of her neck had him away up in the leafy branches of a maple

"*I never saw my cow in such spirits,*" *I said . . . just then she jerked the iron dog from his perch.* (Page 252.)

tree, wondering how he got there **and how he** was going to get down.

Then Traveler—I call her Traveler because she is on **the** road half of the time—went down the turnpike on the run, with the leg of the iron dog swinging **at** the end **of** her leading-strap like a slung-shot, greatly to the annoyance of such **people as she** chanced to knock out with **it.**

Stifling his desire **to** laugh **at my dismay** over the sudden disappearence **of** Comet—I named her Comet because she is so erratic in her movements—my friend, with that delicate courtesy which **is** one of the charms **of high** culture, said, changing the subject **to** relieve my painful confusion:

"This lawn looks **as** though **some wooden-** headed fool had pastured a drove of hogs like himself upon **it. A** hundred dollars won't put **it where** it was half **an** hour **ago, and** where **it** would be now if the fool-killer **had** called on the right man an **hour** ago."

I could **not bear to** see him so distressed **on** my account, so **I** concealed, for the mo- **ment,** my anxiety about Boy—her name is

Boy, because you never know where she is or what she is doing when she is out of your sight—and said, reassuringly:

"Oh, this isn't anything. You should see Thornton's garden. I took her over there with me last evening, and she stayed all night and played with the dog. Thornton has been in bed ever since."

But it didn't seem to cheer him up, and he continued abstracted and constrained in his manner, so I bade him adieu with my usual grave and quiet courtesy, and went home.

A week or two after that, just as I had got Baron well introduced into society—I call her Baron because she is so poor—the man came to me one morning and said she didn't seem to be well. I went to the barn. Beatrice—for it was indeed she—was dead. She was swollen to the size of a sugar hogshead, her neck was broken, an ax was sticking in her head, and there were five or six large perforations in her body. Several bullets were imbedded in the side of her stall, and we found in her feed-box, mixed with her bran, pounded glass, Rough on Rats, and a package of strychnine.

I sent for the cow doctor and a detective. They examined the cow and the premises carefully, and I asked them if they didn't think Julius Cæsar—I called her that because she was dead—had been tampered with. But they said no; she had died a natural death. The cow physician, who knew her well, said he thought she died of old age.

I said, indignantly, that she was only a year old.

But he said that a year was a very long time for some cows to live.

# THE STRIKE AT HINMAN'S

## XIX

WAY back in the fifties, "Hinman's" was not only the best school in Peoria, but it was the greatest school in the world. I sincerely thought so then, and as I was a very lively part of it, I should know. Mr. Hinman was the Faculty, and he was sufficiently numerous to demonstrate cube root with one hand and maintain discipline with the other. Dear old man; boys and girls with grandchildren love him to-day, and think of him among their blessings. He was superintendent of public instruction, board of education, school trustee, county superintendent, principal of the high school and janitor. He

had a pleasant smile, a genius for mathematics, and a West Point idea of obedience and discipline. He carried upon his person a grip that would make the imported malady which mocks that name in these degenerate days, call itself Slack, in very terror at having assumed the wrong title.

We used to have "General Exercises" on Friday afternoon. The most exciting feature of this weekly frivolity consisted of a free-for-all exercise in mental arithmetic. Mr. Hinman gave out lists of numbers, beginning with easy ones and speaking slowly; each succeeding list he dictated more rapidly and with ever-increasing complications of addition, subtraction, multiplication and division, until at last he was giving them out faster than he could talk. One by one the pupils dropped out of the race with despairing faces, but always at the closing peremptory:

"Answer?"

At least a dozen hands shot into the air and as many voices shouted the correct result. We didn't have many books, and the curriculum of an Illinois school in those days was not academic; but two things the children could do, they could spell as well as the dictionary and they could handle figures. Some of the fellows fairly wallowed in them. I didn't. I simply drowned in the shallowest pond of numbers that ever spread itself on the page. As even unto this day I do the same.

Well, one year the Teacher introduced an innovation; "compositions" by the girls and "speakin' pieces" by the boys. It was easy enough for the girls, who had only to read the beautiful thought that "spring is the pleasantest season of the year." Now and then a new girl, from the east, awfully precise, would begin her essay—"spring is the most pleasant season of the year," and her would we call down with derisive laughter, whereat she walked to her seat, very stiffly, with a proud dry-eyed look in her face, only to lay her head upon her desk when she reached it, and weep silently until school closed. But "speakin' pieces" did not meet with favor from the boys, save one or two good boys who were in training by their parents for congressmen or presidents.

The rest of us, who were just boys, with no desire ever to be anything else, endured the tyranny of compulsory oratory about a month, and then resolved to abolish the whole business by a general revolt. Big and little, we agreed to stand by each other, break up the new exercise, and get back to the old order of things—the hurdle races in mental arithmetic and the geographical chants which we could run and intone together.

Was I a mutineer? Well, say, son, your Pa was a constituent conspirator. He was in the color guard. You see, the first boy called on for a declamation was to announce the strike, and as my name stood very high—in the alphabetical roll of pupils—I had an excellent chance of leading the assaulting column, a distinction for which I was not at all ambitious, being a stripling of tender years, ruddy countenance, and sensitive feelings. However, I stiffened the sinews of my soul, girded on my armor by slipping an atlas back under my jacket and was ready for the fray, feeling a little terrified shiver of delight as I thought that the first lick Mr.

Hinman gave me would make him think he had broken my back.

The hour for "speakin' pieces," an hour big with fate, arrived on time. A boy named Aby Abbott was called up ahead of me, but he happened to be one of the presidential aspirants (he was mate on an Illinois river steamboat, stern-wheeler at that, the last I knew of him), and of course he flunked and "said" his piece—a sadly prophetic selection —"Mr. President, it is natural for man to indulge in the illusions of hope." We made such suggestive and threatening gestures at him, however, when Mr. Hinman wasn't looking, that he forgot half his "piece," broke down and cried. He also cried after school, a little more bitterly, and with far better reason.

Then, after an awful pause, in which the conspirators could hear the beating of each other's hearts, my name was called.

I sat still at my desk and said:

"I aint goin' to speak no piece."

Mr. Hinman looked gently surprised and asked:

. . . Then, laying his hand on my shoulder, with most punctilious but chilling courtesy, he invited me to the rostrum. (Page 261.)

"Why not, Robert?"

I replied :

" Because there ain't goin' to be **any** more speakin' pieces."

The teacher's eyes grew round and big **as** he inquired :

"Who says there will not?"

I said, **in** slightly firmer tones, as I realized that the moment had come **for** dragging the rest of the rebels **into** court :

" All of us boys !"

But Mr. Hinman smiled, **and** said quietly that he guessed there would be " a little more speaking before the close of the session." Then laying his **hand on** my shoulder, with most punctilious but chilling courtesy, he invited **me** to the rostrum. The " rostrum " was **twenty-five** feet distant, **but I** arrived there on schedule time and only touched my feet to the floor twice on **my** way.

And then **and** there, under **Mr.** Hinman's judicious coaching, before the assembled school, with feelings, nay, emotions which I now shudder **to** recall, I did my first " song **and** dance." **Many** times before had I stepped off a solo-cachuca to the staccato pleasing of a fragment of slate frame, upon which my tutor was a gifted performer, but never until that day did I accompany myself with words. Boy like, I had chosen for my '' piece '' a poem sweetly expressive of those peaceful virtues which I most heartily despised. So that my performance, at the inauguration of the strike, as Mr. Hinman conducted the overture, ran something like this—

" Oh, not for me (whack) is the rolling (whack) drum,
    Or the (whack, whack) trumpet's wild (whack)
        appeal ! (Boo-hoo !)
  Or the cry (swish—whack) of (boo-hoo-hoo !) war
        when the (whack) foe is come (ouch !)
    Or the (ow—wow !) brightly (whack) flashing
        (whack-whack) steel ! (wah-hoo, wah-hoo !) "

Words and symbols can not convey to the most gifted imagination the gestures with which I illustrated the seven stanzas of this beautiful poem. I had really selected it to please my mother, whom I had invited to be present, when I supposed I would deliver it. But the fact that she attended a missionary meeting in the Baptist church that afternoon made me a friend of missions forever. Suffice it to say, then, that my pantomime kept pace and time with Mr. Hinman's system of punctuation until the last line was sobbed and whacked out. I groped my bewildered way to my seat through a mist of tears and sat down gingerly and sideways, inly wondering why an inscrutable providence had given to the rugged rhinoceros the hide which the eternal fitness of things had plainly prepared for the school-boy.

But I quickly forgot my own sorrow and dried my tears with laughter in the enjoyment of the subsequent acts of the opera, as the chorus developed the plot and action. Mr. Hinman, who had been somewhat gentle with me, dealt firmly with the larger boy who followed, and there was a scene of revelry for the next twenty minutes. The old man shook Bill Morrison until his teeth rattled so you couldn't hear him cry. He hit Mickey McCann, the tough boy from the Lower Prairie, and Mickey ran out and lay down in the snow to cool off. He hit Jake

Bailey across the legs with a slate frame, and it hurt so that Jake couldn't howl—he just opened his mouth wide, held up his hands, gasped, and forgot his own name. He pushed Bill Haskell into a seat and the bench broke.

He ran across the room and reached out for Lem Harkins, and Lem had a fit before the old man touched him. He shook Dan Stevenson for two minutes, and when he let him go, Dan walked around his own desk five times before he could find it, and then he couldn't sit down without holding on. He whipped the two Knowltons with a skate-strap in each hand at the same time; the Greenwood family, five boys and a big girl, he whipped all at once with a girl's skipping rope, and they raised such a united wail that the clock stopped.

He took a twist in Bill Rodecker's front hair, and Bill slept with his eyes open for a week. He kept the atmosphere of that school-room full of dust, and splinters, and lint, weeping, wailing and gnashing of teeth, until he reached the end of the alphabet and all hearts ached and wearied of the inhuman strife and wicked contention. Then he stood up before us, a sickening tangle of slate frame, strap, ebony ferule and skipping rope, a smile on his kind old face, and asked, in clear, triumphant tones:

"WHO says there isn't going to be any more speaking pieces?"

And every last boy in that school sprang to his feet; standing there as one human being with one great mouth, we shrieked in concerted anguish:

"NOBODY DON'T!"

And your Pa, my son, who led that strike, has been "speakin' pieces" ever since.

# CANTISTOPTHIS.

THE Parson of a Struggling Church was lying in his bed; three months' arrears of salary was pillowing his head. His couch was strewn with trades-men's bills that pricked his heart like thorns, and nearly all life's common ills were goading him like horns.

The Deacon sat beside him as the moments ticked away, and bent his head to catch the words the Parson had to say:

"If I never shall arise from this hard bed on which I lie, if my warfare is accomplished and it's time for me to die, take a message to the janitor before I pass away—tell him fires are for December and the windows are for May.   Tell him when he lays the notices upon the pulpit's height, to shove them, neath the cushion, far out of reach and sight. And when he hears the preacher's voice, in whispers soft expire, that is the time to slam the door and rattle at the fire.

"And the Deacons—tell the Deacons too, through all the busy week to hang their boots up in the sun to hatch a Sunday squeak. With steel shod canes to poke the man who comes to church to snore, and use the boys who laugh in church to mop the vestry floor.

"There's another, too, the Woman who talks the sermon through; tell her I do not mind her buzz—my hearing days are few. Tell her to leave her mouth at home, some Sunday, for a minute, and listen to a text, at least, without a whisper in it.

"And tell the Board of Trustees not to weep with bitter tears, for I can't be any deader now than they have been for years. And tell half my congregation that I'm glad salvation's free, for that's the only chance for them between the desk and me.

"And a farewell to the choir! How the

name my memory racks! If they could get
up their voices as they do get up their backs!
—Why, the stars would join their music and
the welkin would rejoice, while the happy
congregation could not hear a single voice.
But tell them I forgive them, and Oh! Tell
them that I said that I wanted them to come
and sing above me—When I'm Dead!"

His voice grew faint and hoarser, but it
gave a laughing break, a kind of gurgling
chuckle as a minister might make. But the
Deacon rose up slowly, and sternly he looked
down upon the Parson's twinkling eyes with
most portentous frown. And he stiffly said
"Good morning," as he walked off in his
ire, for the Deacon was the leader of that
amiable choir.

## THE END.

www.ingramcontent.com/pod-product-compliance
Lightning Source LLC
Chambersburg PA
CBHW060524030726
47498CB00004B/1073